Ahead Of My Time

Kendra Armstrong

I want to Thank all my family and friends who inspired me to continue to write and I want to Thank everyone who supported me with your interest in my book.

An expert in anything was once a beginner-

Helen Hayes

Chapter 1

Teenage Rebellion

Really? All I heard was the sound of a muffled alarm clock beeping down the hall.

Why didn't Grandma wake me up this morning?

Gosh I have to do everything around here. I'm still tired, that party last night didn't stop jumping until 3am. Most of all the high school kids had left at midnight complaining about school, so I party hard with the college kids; which is mainly who I party with anyway.

I went in the bathroom to take my curlers out my sandy brown shoulder length hair. I already set my clothes out before I fell out so I threw on a pair of hip hugger jeans that fit my size 14 frame perfect, then a belly shirt to show off the new belly ring I picked up from the mall Saturday. I apply my makeup real good around my hazel brown eyes to give that natural look to my already flawless mocha brown skin and put on a pair of my favorite stilettos to accentuate my sexy feminine walk. My grandma always says I look like a hooker that I'm going to attract the wrong kind of attention I always ignore her, besides it's not the 1950's anymore you got to show a lot of skin to fit in.

I head out the room and see grandma getting out of bed, finally pushing the snooze button on the alarm clock.

"I'm already up grandma so you can lie back down," I sound annoyed.

She yawns a bit, "You don't want any breakfast sweetie?"

"No grandma I will grab something on my way to school," I say walking past her bedroom.

I was kind of thinking of ditching today but since it was Monday, and I didn't feel like hearing grandma's mouth so, I just went.

Grandma has been taking care of me since I was nine my mom died of a drug overdose, and my dad never was in the picture, but grandma worked all her life, so we lived in a nice rural area, and since she's retired now I'm more on her radar than I used to be; It just had to start in my senior year.

I jumped in my little two door sedan and headed to the coffee shop to grab a donut and some coffee before school, I much rather pass on school food.

I pull in front of the local coffee house called The Grind House its right down the street from the school. I get to the front counter to see Trey the coffee guy a little nickname I gave him.

"Good morning Ace you want your usual?"

I glance over the menu for a while even though I could about recite it because I've been here so many times.

"I don't know I'm thinking I need to lay off the donuts starting to get a little pudgy," while I'm patting my stomach.

"Yeah right you got to be 150lbs tops," which he did get it about right but a girl still needs to watch her figure.

"Why thank you for noticing and yeah just give me the usual."

As he reached over to grab the money I stroked his hand a bit which caused the customer behind me to clear her throat, like that would speed me up.

I grabbed my coffee and rolled my eyes at the girl while I headed for the door. I jump in my car and did a straight shot down the street to school. Since The Grind House was right down the street most of the kids came there after school to socialize.

I head in the school in a hurry because of the usually flirting with Trey that ran a little longer as well as the late night I had. I didn't bother to stop at my locker I just headed to class. My first period is literature with Mr. Mayhue.

I'm stopped by Natalie she's one of my good friends well really my only friend, females tend to be jealous of me. I don't run in a click it's just me and Natalie, although she has friends other than me. We have been friends ever since me and grandma moved here. After my mom died grandma said a fresh start is what we needed. So when I started school here that's when I met Natalie and we have been friends ever since.

 Most people tend to think I'm a bad influence on Natalie, but the teachers only hoped that her good behavior would rub off on me. Well since it's the last year of high school for us they might as well stop hoping.

"You know Mr. Mayhue will not let you in his class with that on," she says with sass.

Sometimes I do get carried away with my looks but I can't help it if I'm beautiful.

"Well I don't have anything else so if he doesn't like it he can shove it where the sun doesn't shine."

Both of us broke out in laughter. So we made it to his class just as the bell rung.

Mr. Mayhue noticed me instantly.

"Miss Bellows," He said looking me up and down. "Are you in a club or a classroom?"

He kinda put me on the spot which pissed me off but I answered anyway, maybe a little too smart.

"When I got up this morning I did intend on going to the club but I thought maybe I should get my education first."

Some of the kids in the class started to chuckle, so I think that made him a bit upset.

He got up from his chair and slammed his class planner on the desk making a lot of the kid's jump, "well Miss Bellows you either change or get out my class!"

God he doesn't have to be such an ass but I guess he can't help it.

I got up from my seat, "You don't have to tell me twice, I'm gone."

But Natalie grabbed my hand, "I have a t-shirt in my locker you know the combo just change, stop being such a baby," she whispered the last part.

I stumped out the class, sometimes I can be a baby but I'm a person who does like to get her way.

So I head to Natalie's locker. Everything is in its place no trash, books lined up neatly, and no food; she's always such a neat freak. There it was on the top shelf a plan white t a little big but it will do.

I do need to keep good grade in Mr. Mayhue's class after all he's one of the easier subjects I have .Most people think because I act like this I'm dumb but little do they know. I need to pass 5 out of my 6 classes every semester or I won't walk with my class, school has only been in for a week and I'm already on most of the teachers shit list, but to be honest I really don't care I have all year to make up for it.

I head in the bathroom to put the shirt on, I only put it over my other shirt, I could have done that in the hallway but I don't need any more reasons to get in trouble.

As I'm pulling the shirt down over my head I glance out the window, it was a man standing across the parking lot of the school, just staring at the school. Was he looking through the window? No way. It was way too far. I walked closer to the small window in the front of the bathroom there was no way he could see me, but it sure looked like it so I hurried and exited the bathroom because it really gave me the creeps.

Mr. Mayhue looked up from his planner as I was entering the classroom, "nice of you to join us Miss Bellows.

I just gave him an evil look and took a seat next to Natalie and worded Thank you.

Mr. Mayhue was giving a lecture of the early 1900's and how women were more stay at home moms and the men did all the working. That couldn't be me I not letting any man knock me up and leave me at home.

Chapter 2

The Grind House

Finally school was over so Natalie and I headed over to The Grind House for a refill on coffee. I was hoping to see Trey, but his shift was usually over before we got out of school.

Natalie lectured me the whole way there about what I wore to Mr. Mayhue's class it was only a 5 minute drive but I could swear it was an hour the way she talked.

"Stacy you know how Mr. Mayhue is you need to watch what you wear, and how you talk, or he will have you expelled, he's given you far too many chances and we're only in the second week of school."

Who cares he can't do anything to me but I agreed just to shut her up.

"Your right I will be cautions next time," I lied.

We walked in the coffee shop to see it already loaded with tons of kids from school, great a long wait so me and Natalie sat at a table in the corner with a view of outside. I sat down for a minute then walked over as it started to shorten.

"Hey Natalie you want your usual?" I yelled over my shoulder.

"Yeah Thanks!"

I walked over to the line and turned when I heard someone calling me.

"Hey Ace!"

It was Ronny one of the jocks from school a real asshole; he's been trying to get in my pants all summer but like I told him you don't have nothing to offer me so don't even think about it, but I still politely waved back.

I made it up to the front to be greeted by a familiar face.

"What in the world are you doing here?" I shrieked obviously a little excited.

"Hey Ace," the sound of Trey's smooth voice had my lady parts quivering,

"Overtime our afternoon girl called in sick just my luck," he smiled.

I loved looking at this man; Trey is a medium build, about 5'10, 5'11, deep brown eyes, caramel complexion, with dark brown hair cut evenly to his head even though we flirted everyday he never tried to ask me out, probably because of the age difference he's 21 and I'm 17 but I'm gonna snag him even if it's just for one night of fun.

"Well just give me my usual coffee and Natalie's too she's over there in the corner."

He peeked around the other customers to give Natalie a friendly wave.

"When things die down you have to come and sit with us for a minute I would love the extra company," I smiled.

He politely smiled back revealing a row of perfectly groomed teeth to go with that gorgeous smile.

We sat in the corner for a good while Natalie was doing some of her homework, and my phone kept buzzing I looked at the caller ID it was grandma I swear she's a stalker.

Natalie looked up from her English book giving me a disapproving look, "you need to answer that before she worries Stacy."

Sometimes I wonder why I'm friends with Natalie she is so by the book then I realize she looks good in some jeans. So going out with her is so fun because we are so hot and besides she has been my friend since we were 10.

Natalie' s about 5'5, black hair shoulder length but she always wears it in a bun, hazel eyes and mocha complexion with a size 14 body to die for but you wouldn't know it because she always covers it, only when we are going out to the club which wouldn't be much if I left it up to her.

I picked up the phone. "Hello," In my annoyed voice.

 "Stacy why in the world haven't you called me back or even answered my many phone calls?" Grandma squealed.

"I'm busy grandma I will call you back," Then I closed the phone shut.

I looked over to Natalie, "you happy now?"

Natalie looked up from her book again, "You know I love you but the way you treat your grandma is going to bite you in the ass, just you wait and see."

I just rolled my eyes and continued to stare out the window.

The time seemed to fly by and we were in the coffee house a good three hours and they were getting ready to close up.

"Well you ready Stacy I'm done with my homework."

"I'm waiting for Trey to get a chance to come over here."

"Oh my god give it up Stacy he's not into you like you would like just because you flaunt that ass of yours around doesn't mean every man will jump."

"Really? I swear I smell hate, how about you just leave your dampening the mood anyways."

"You were my ride here," She panicked.

"Well there's a new invention it's called a bus."

With that said she stormed out of there, she was ruining my moment but maybe I was just a little bit bitchy so I get up to go after her when Trey calls me.

"Hey Ace can I still join you guys?"

He's walking over looking good as ever.

"I got a few minutes before we totally close."

"Oh yeah come…. Sit."

"Hey where's Natalie were you guys leaving?"

"Not at all Natalie had to get home curfew and all."

It wasn't quite a lie she did need to go!!

We sat down and chatted for a few minutes before the rest of the tables started to clear out and I was the only one left in the coffee house it wasn't all that late maybe around 7 but because it was fall it got dark quicker.

"Hey if it's getting late you can head out," He says.

Such a gentleman but I on the other hand don't have a curfew and grandma will just nag that I missed dinner something I can ignore.

"I can wait till you're done cleaning," I blushed.

So I watched him clean the tables and usually I wouldn't give a man so much attention but something about Trey had me going. Trey closed shop and we conversed a little more, the employees waved goodbye as they left; it was only two since the girl that usually closed called in.

So we engaged in more conversation while he closed up shop he asked me if I ever thought about working. I kinda wanted to laugh at that because I don't need to work I get what I want from grandma or a stupid guy thinking he was going to get something out of me but I wasn't going to tell him that I wanted him for my right now new boo.

I swear he was so handsome, funny, and smart he talked about his college classes, he's studying in medical and a few side associate degrees he usually takes them in the afternoon that's why he works early mornings but being a manager he has to fill in when someone calls in, any women would be lucky to have him just not me I really am not the tie down kind of girl.

I looked outside it was late and even though grandma probably fell asleep on the couch waiting up for me I didn't want to hear her mouth.

"I had so much fun chattin' with you but I got to get home grandma would be worried."

"No problem I completely understand I will walk you to your car."

Then he locked up the store, walked me to the car, opened the door for me, like I said a real gentleman he caught me off guard with a peck on the cheek but it felt like he left hot coal burning, then chills went down my spine, Wow!

I got in the car and watched him get in his car then he gave me a wave while I was glancing at my phone 9pm damn where did the time go not to mention I had about 6 missed calls from grandma. I looked up and he already pulled away. I turned the ignition. *Plunk plunk.*

"Oh my God," I said out loud.

I tried it again and nothing, I know I had gas, and I maintenance my car on a regular. Why did Trey have to drive off first? I know he probably knew a little about cars he probably seen me looking down at my phone and figured I was okay. Why couldn't I start my car up first?

"Damn. Damn. Damn it!!" I yelled.

I turned quickly when I heard footsteps, yah he came back but when I looked up it was a familiar face just not Trey's. I scramble to lock the door it was the guy who I know I saw staring at the school.

He approaches the car slowly like you would see the killer in a scary movie flick but I already locked the doors so he just stares at me from a distance for what it seems like for hours. His piercing pitch black eyes staring into my soul. I finally had enough of the staring contest so I grab my cell phone to call 911 but all I hear is crash, I duck my head down to avoid the glass from getting in my face when I drop my phone, I scramble to get it but I feel glass sticking me and his big burly hands grabbing me and pulling me out the window. I screamed but I know everything is closed down in this area. I'm still screaming, kicking and moving my arms as he places one arm over my nose and face with a tissue and the other arm grasping me firmly, but I find myself getting tired and out of breath then.......

I came to with a headache. I tried to open my eyes but felt dizzy. I kept fluttering them open trying to remember where I was I moved around, and noticed I was in a bed how did I get home damn Stacy you drank too much again. I finally opened my eyes, but it was nothing familiar about the room. Then all my memories came flooding back.

"Oh my god the man," I screamed.

I felt around for my cell phone, and then I jumped out the bed. I immediately came crashing back down it must had been the effects of what the man gave me. I think it's called chloroform; I really thought that was just in movies. I set in place for a minute to stop from being dizzy, while I was doing that I notice I was in a huge room it was a dresser, and a nightstand a set it looked old though and a lazy boy in the corner. I couldn't really make out much else because the room was dark, but I could see the moonlight shining through the window. I finally stood up and I stood there for a moment so I wouldn't fall back again and walked over to the window. I tried to bang on it but it seemed to be made of some type of plastic, not glass I banged, and banged but nothing I was so tired from screaming at the top of my lungs, I sat down on the floor by the side of the bed.

Then I heard a noise, "It's useless no one can hear you so stop banging but if you feel you need to continue I know how to put bad girls in their place."

A shiver ran down my spine I looked around but I didn't see anyone but the room was dark and I was afraid to even move so I set there and did nothing more curled up in a ball with tears streaming down my face.

Chapter 3

Reform Me?

I woke up with my throat dry from all the crying and my body stiff from sleeping up right in the corner I got up to stretch a little my eyes couldn't adjust just yet it was still dark outside I wonder how long I was sleep? I looked out the window again to try and get a glimpse of where I was but nothing looked familiar just dirt roads but I could make out a shadow of a house a few feet away a huge house.

I was scared to even leave the room just in case the man was nearby. What did he want from me? I know grandma would be worried by now then again I've stayed out so many times that she's probably sleeping away on the couch.

I heard a knock. It was my door who was it I ducked back down by the side of the bed then there it was again the knob twisted and someone pushed the door open. First I couldn't make out the silhouette but then I realized it was a girl she stepped in the room and flipped the light on. She was about my height 5'5, dark red hair past her shoulders, emerald green eyes and---I gasped she looked to be about 9 months pregnant besides being pregnant she reminded me of Ariel the little mermaid.

"Don't be afraid I won't hurt you," holding her hands in the air as a gesture she was safe.

I still sat in the same spot I didn't know who she was or what she wanted from me but I wasn't about to go near her but she edge closer to me.

"I heard you crying do you need anything? Some water; are you hungry?

I just stared at her I didn't know what to say she was offering me food that probably was poisoned but if they wanted to kill me I don't think he would have brought me here or would he?

"Who are you?" I said in a dry shaky voice that I wondered did she even hear me.

"I'm Amy," she replied sweetly then continued. "I know you probably wondering why you are here."

I shook my head my mouth was too dry to say another word.

"Come on lets go to the kitchen I will get you some water."

I reluctantly got up I was still scared but something about Amy made me trust her. The floor was cold as I didn't have on any shoes on I guess wearing stilettos wasn't a good idea as I probably couldn't out ran him.

So I followed her out the room and realized we were in a one level house as soon as you walk out the room you see another bedroom across the hall and a bathroom down the hall to the right, a spacious kitchen connected to a small dining room, and a living area with a couch, loveseat, and a small box TV.

She leads me in the kitchen and grabs a plastic cup out the cabinet and turns on the faucet to fill then hands it to me I hadn't realized I was shaking until I had the cup in my hand I managed to get a few sips before it dropped. She hurried to clean it up.

"I'm sorry," I managed to get out but she was bending down sopping up the water with a towel.

I looked around some more and realized there weren't windows anywhere else just in the room I was in. Then I heard the voice again, "Amy have you made you new sister comfortable?"

I started shaking even more and burst out crying and ran for the nearest corner.

"Hi pa, she is a little scared but things are going okay."

I didn't know what was going on was that her father why are they doing this to me? Before I knew it Amy was by my side, "get away from me what do you crazy freaks want from me?"

"Will you let me explain?"

"That's all I've been waiting for."

"What's your name?"

"Stacy Bellows."

"Okay Stacy that's not really my father but he instructs us to call him pa."

"Us how many are in here? I only seen one other room besides the one I was in."

I started to panic all kinds of weird thoughts went through my head he's a serial kidnapper he took me, Amy and whoever else.

"There were more but……..,"she trailed off but what did but mean she seemed sadden by the thought of it.

"All I can tell you obey all his rules and he won't kill you," she said the last part in a whisper as though I didn't hear her.

"What do you mean kill me?"

"Stacy Pa is old fashioned he doesn't like the way women dress now and days he thinks you attract the wrong kind of people although he does see how you were raised and that's a factor in how he picks us."

I just looked at her I didn't have anything to say I wanted her to finish. Then she cleared her throat and continued.

"If you had a parent or grandparent who raises you and you still disrespect them and they are doing the best they can he doesn't like that ; he doesn't like disobedient children," her face froze with that reference.

So he's been watching me to know how I act, how long? It only made me more worried but Amy continued to tell me everything that I needed to know to stay alive and I listened.

I hated to ask but how in the world would she just bow down and stay it had to be more to it but I wasn't going to go down without a fight.

"You never tried to escape?"

She looked over at me and seemed worried like the darkness fell then she looked at me with the saddest eyes.

"I guess you weren't listening Stacy there's no escaping and now you will learn why so few survive."

I was stumped what was she talking about but she walked past me straight into her room and closed the door. What was that all about I was still afraid to get up why would she just leave mid-sentence this is crazy I got up off the floor and took in my surroundings again then I heard a door open but I was looking right at hers and it wasn't hers so I turned and seen horror.

"So you want to escape? I hear everything, nothing gets passed me."

I ran as fast as I could to Amy's door banged and banged but when she wouldn't open it I darted for the room I was in and looked around. I jumped in the closet backing skittishly against the wall and cried what was he going to do to me?

I heard footsteps coming closer and closer and soon the door swung open. He dragged me out by my hair slamming my head into the wall. I felt dizzy and started giving me a beating as I never had I thought I was going to die. A slap in the face then he just kept kicking and kicking me until I started spitting up blood. When my body finally went limp he leaned over and said, "Pa doesn't like disobedient children," then I blacked out.

I woke up to the chill of cold water on my body but also to excruciating pain. I was sitting upright in a shower with Amy bent over me wiping my wounds and cleaning my body. I could barely talk but she just hushed me and continued to clean me. Once she was done she helped me walk to the bedroom where she helped me dress and laid me too bed.

She sat by the side of me rubbing me softly, "I'm sorry this had to happen but you cannot disobey him he will kill you so just keep quiet and live."

I managed to get out a few words before my voice completely went out.

"What does he want from us?"

She looked into my eyes and in the fiercest voice she said, "To reform us or kill us," and with those words a single tear slid down my cheek and I drifted off.

Chapter 4

Broken

I woke with the sun shining high in the sky. I couldn't move at all he beat me so bad I don't think I would be able to walk for days I tried to move but it hurt far too much. I didn't have to get out the bed anyways because I heard the door, my heart nearly dropped I thought it was him but it wasn't it was another guy standing in the door way I didn't know what to expect was he here to finish me off for disobeying.

"Don't be alarmed I won't hurt you I'm like you I'm Amy's husband Kyle."

Like me?

Stuck in the bed half beaten to death? Not like me by far.

I didn't know what to think he takes men too what the heck is going on but it did give me some kind of relief to know the baby didn't belong to him or did it I will ask when I can stomach the answer.

"Where's Amy?"

"She's resting the baby is due any time and I don't want her over doing it."

"Hey…..where were you last night?" My words stumbled a little.

I hadn't seen him none last night and the little house isn't big at all where could he have been?

"I work."

What... I screamed inside. He gets out but comes back. He gets out but doesn't send the cops. What is wrong with these people? He picked the right ones but when he got me his kidnapping days are coming to an end.

I didn't know what to say I didn't want to say the wrong thing and he comes back and finishes me off so for now I'm going to play his little game to save my life and give me time to come up with a plan.

"So where do you work?"

He looked at me puzzled like he didn't want to say the wrong thing too but answered anyway.

"I work at the house cleaning and doing maintenance work for Pa."

He said it like it was something to be proud of. I left it at that and continued to squirm around in the bed trying to find a comfortable position to lie in but every time I moved one way I nearly broke out in tears.

"I think something might be broke."

"Its punishment, he will make you suffer through the pain until you learn."

His eyes gazed around the room as though he was looking for something. I gazed with him but nothing.

"If you need anything just yell I won't be far."

He walked out the room and shut the door to leave me in my thoughts. I wondered if granny reported me missing. It is well into the next day and I always came home.

Thoughts of Trey entered my mind. I wondered was he expecting me this morning to get my coffee. Then I remembered my car I know they would be looking for me he took me right in front of the coffee house. It shouldn't be any time before they get evidence and find me. I felt a relief wash over me things were looking up.

My stomach started to growl I was starving. I really didn't want to call Amy and that guy still freaked me out. Who just leaves and comes back and doesn't tell anyone? I moved around again but screams of agony only seeped out. Something is broken, and then Kyle came running in the room.

"You okay?"

"I'm fine I just tried to move and realized something is broke."

"Did you need something?"

"Yeah I am kind of hungry."

"I can get you something because Amy's having some cravings too," He said in a chuckling tone.

How in the hell can they joke in a time like this maybe because they have been here far too long but I don't know exactly how long I wonder does he keep us forever?

"So when's the baby's exact due date?"

"Well she hasn't seen a doctor but we're guessing in about two weeks or so but anytime really."

I'm not the mothering type, I'm the noisy type and I want all the information I can get to get the hell out of here.

"So how do you know if everything is okay?"

"Pa is trained medic he comes in once a week to check on her he even has an ultrasound machine so we know it's a boy."

Great what can't this monster do?

He excused himself to the kitchen to fix something to eat. I could tell he knew what he was doing because I could smell the aroma of eggs and bacon coming from there it made my stomach growl even louder. He left the door open so when he delivered Amy's food I could see him walk past.

"I will be right back with yours he yelled passing the doorway."

He was a nice looking man dark brown hair and brown eyes he was tall also somewhere around 6ft tall, his skin was light and toned, he had thick full lips with straight pearly white teeth when he smiled, he was groomed very well to be a kidnapped victim.

"Sorry for the wait Amy has been real ornery."

"It's okay I don't mind it didn't take you long anyways you must be a pro."

He placed the well scrambled eggs, crispy bacon, and buttered toast on a tray in front of me with two plastic cups one with orange juice and the other with milk I'm thinking he didn't know what I wanted.

"I forgot to ask you what you wanted to drink so I brought you both."

"It's okay I'm thirsty I'll probably drink both."

I'm glad he didn't mess up my face because I would hate to eat food out of a straw. He turned to leave the room.

"Hey I don't have nothing to eat with," but as starved as I was I probably would have dug in with my hands

"Oh I forgot!!"

He reached in his pocket and handed me a napkin rolled up with plastic utensils in them I guess Pa has his entire basis covered because that would have been my first thought to stab him and get the hell out of here.

So for the fact that I can't move and who knows how long that's going to last he has me beat. I finish everything up and grab the tray and leant over to the side of the bed to place it on the floor and every part of me is stiff and in pain tears roll down my cheek.

I begin to feel sleepy as I sat in the bed like my body was giving out without my permission then I started to hear voices as my body heavily slumps in the bed.

"Pa I put the pain medicine in her drink and the sleeping pills as well."

"Good as soon as she is out I will look her over and make sure she has no broken bones."

I try to fight the medicine but it just isn't happening I didn't want his creepy crawly hands on me at all but my body was failing me and I was drifting off I started to cry because I was scared of what he would do to me while I was out.

I woke up to a dark room mouth dry and stomach rumbling and my leg was in a cast I could barely see or move I searched my body I was in the same night ware but I had body wrap on my chest but I wasn't in as much pain as before. Time seemed to have slipped away I must have slept the whole day away so now it's night again.

I swung my leg off the bed I knew how to move I broke my leg once before when I was in 7th grade. I made my way to the bathroom that was on the other side of my room once I was done I hopped out the room to see Amy in the Kitchen.

She spun around to greet me.

"Hey sleepy head you shouldn't be walking around come take a seat."

She helped me over to the dining room to the table to take a seat in one of the 4 chairs that sat there around the table.

"I guess Kyle is working? What time is it anyway?"

She looked at me quietly trying to find the words to say with a sincere look on her face.

"You have been out for 3 days."

I thought I heard wrong but I asked again anyways.

"Say what?"

"You have been out for 3 days it's Thursday night Pa gave you drugs and pain killer to put you out because you were in a lot of pain as well as you had some fractured ribs, and leg but otherwise your okay."

I swear right now I could kill her he is the one who did it to me in the first place and then he looks over me like someone off the street beat me up what is wrong with these people I'm leaving NOW.

"He did this to me and you act like he did me a favor what's wrong with you?" I was angry at this point I was shouting.

"I know you're mad and hurt but Stacy if you don't shut up right now this will be our last conversation."

At this point I didn't really care I wanted out of here rather I'm dead or alive I'm not going to stay in here and obey this lunatic.

I got up and hopped for the door it was metal and looked like it was bolted shut I started banging on it and crying I wanted someone to get me out of here.

"Stop it, Stop it, Stacy!!"

I could hear Amy shouting but I didn't care he either is going to kill me or let me go. Soon enough I heard the door being unlocked but I couldn't move away quick enough and it swung open and hit me so I fell to the floor.

"I've had enough of this whining baby you don't value life so I will put you out of your misery."

I could hear Amy in the background begging for my life what does she care she doesn't even know me?

"Pa no she doesn't know any better please I will train her please give her one more chance."

"My most obedient daughter is begging for your life you spoiled brat."

Then whack right across the face.

"This is for her; if I hear you again no one will be able to save you."

Then he turned and walked out locking the door behind him. I sat there on the floor crying.

"Why did you do that I wish I was dead who just wants to be a prisoner all their life?

I used the wall behind me to get up off the floor and started hopping back to the room.

"Rather you realize it or not no one will ever find you and the sooner you realize that your chances of survival are greater."

I was a survivor rather she realized it or not and I wasn't going to let neither one of them break me. I made it to the room door and slammed it in that crazy bitches face.

Chapter 5

I'm no Midwife

Days became weeks and all hope of anyone finding me was lost I sat in the room crying day and night refusing to eat and slowly killing myself it was becoming too much to handle. So one night I got up out the bed I was now able to walk on my leg since it was a simple fracture, went into the kitchen to make me something to eat I was hoping Amy was sleep. I was able to walk but was still weak since I hadn't eaten in a week. I quickly made a sandwich and was heading back into the room when I heard Amy moaning.

I knew Kyle was at the house working so I crept to the door and it was cracked open she was in the bed holding her stomach.

I whispered. "Oh my goodness it must be time."

"Stacy is that you?" She was panting heavily.

I pushed the door open and went in I never really seen the room it was decorated nice, a lot nicer than mine it had powder blue walls, navy blue curtain it had one window like my room, white carpet with a multi- color blue area rug, and the bed spread was checkered blue and in the corner of the room a wood crib with dark blue and brown bedding with green frogs on it.

I inched my way into the room.

"Yes it's me Amy, are you okay?"

"I…I think it's time" She was barely able to catch her breath.

I didn't know what to do when a baby was being born never did I want kids or like them, I never babysat for money, or goggled at the sight of a baby and here I was in a room with a lady who is about to push out one at anytime now.

"What do I do?"

"Pa…. he should be here soon I know he should be able to hear me but in the meanwhile get some towels out my bathroom and wet a wash cloth for me."

I ran into their bathroom got as many towels as I could find, ran some cold water, wet the towel and ran back out the room. I started moving the blanket off the bed and noticed it was wet so I pulled the sheets and everything from up under her, put all the pillows in back of her and placed the dry towels under her moving her legs carefully. She let out another louder moan and I placed the towel to her forehead to wipe the sweat.

"I need to push," Her breathing was now calmer.

"What?"

"I feel him he is right there."

"I think you should wait for someone who knows what they are doing."

"I trust you, please Stacy I can't do this alone."

I was totally grossed out about the situation but I did it anyway. I spread her legs open as far as they could pulled up the night gown and there, she was right a little patch of light red hair peaking so I did like the movies.

"Push, push Amy!"

She grunted and panted and pushed and pushed I could see him sliding out more and more.

She fell back in the bed for a few minutes gasping for air.

"Okay I think one more push and he should be out."

So I grabbed one of the extra towels and she did one last push and I placed my hand under his head and pulled him free I wrapped him tight in the towel and handed him to Amy who was breathing slowly.

"You did it Amy he's here."

She smile at him and then fainted I grabbed the baby I didn't know what to do the umbilical cord was still attached I didn't want to cut it nor did I know how and then that's when I heard the shuffling.

Pa and Kyle came running in the room I was holding the baby when Pa came up to the bed with a black bag filled with medical supplies. I flinched when he opened the towel to cut the cord then he wrapped him back up that's when I got up and handed the baby to Kyle. I backed slowly back to the door since they were busy I thought it was a perfect time to escape I knew it was wrong to leave Amy like that but I had to think I me I inched back further and further while he was working Amy over I could hear him.

"She lost a lot of blood but I'm going to start her on some fluids she should be fine childbirth is tiresome."

I finally inched out the room and ran for the door that was locked I wasn't going to let it defeat me though I slowly walked back to room to see Pa coming out of it he had a look of joy on his face that scared the crap out of me.

"Another boy he will do his Pa proud."

I moved back against the wall but I don't even think he noticed me but then her turned and smile.

"You did a fine job Stacy maybe there is hope for you."

Then he went out the door and locked it. I went back into the room to see Kyle sitting on the bed beside a still passed out Amy.

"What's wrong with her?" I asked Kyle.

"Pa says she is very tired but he has hopes she will be okay he's going to get fluids for an IV."

He didn't sound too convinced.

I walked up to him and could see in his eyes he was terrified and for the first time I see why his loyalty lied in Pa he had his family in his hands.

"Go clean the baby off I will tend to Amy."

I took all the wet things off the bed including slipping her night clothes off placed them on the floor and cleaned her. I hurried to put her things on because I didn't know how long Pa would be once that was done Kyle place the baby in the crib so he could hold Amy while I put clean sheets on the bed. I made the bed as neat as possible and he placed her gently back into the bed then he sat down next to her stroking her cheek.

I walked over to the crib to look at the baby I had to admit he was beautiful, light green eyes; light red hair baby smooth skin and he just lie there sleeping away not knowing the horrors of his life. I glanced back at Kyle who was now laying his head across Amy's chest talking to her I could barely make out what he was saying but what I did hear scared me.

"I didn't plan on this."

I quickly turned my head so he wouldn't notice me.

"So what's his name?" I yelled out making sure he didn't notice I was looking.

"Amy says a boy should be named after his father so we decided on Kyle Jr. but KJ for short."

I could tell he was starting to cry his voice cracked when he talked, he really loved her and was scared for her life.

I waited by the crib for a while just staring down at KJ I don't know why I was so fascinated with him I didn't even like kids but he just looked so innocent sleeping there. Kyle just put a diaper on him and wrapped him back in a small receiving blanket.

Pa arrived soon after with formula and started putting Amy's IV in she still lie their sleeping peacefully.

"Stacy feed the baby. I much rather him be breast fed but because of the circumstances formula will do."

I looked at him like he was crazy feed the baby I didn't know the first thing about that.

"Did you hear me girl?" He yelled the question my way which startled the baby and he started to cry.

"I... Don't know how," I stumbled over the words scared he would do something to me so I picked up KJ and tried to calm him down.

"Young women these days don't know a thing about being a good mother."

"I'm sorry Pa I will figure it out," I rushed out the room with baby in tow to make him a bottle.

I didn't even recognize myself bowing down to that man.

I picked up the formula and I read the instructions and proceeded to making him a bottle while soothing him in my arms once I found the bottle and boiled the water I sat in the dining room chair and eased the bottle in his mouth he instantly started sucking and calmed down.

"Wow wasn't as hard as I thought."

"I know you just have to have a passion for life and today you got a taste of it," Pa approached me looking down at KJ.

I wanted to grab that pot of boiling water and throw it at him.

As close as he was I felt a surge of protection sore through me to protect KJ even though he wasn't mine he was still innocent and I had to protect him at all cost.

He didn't come any closer I think he noticed my reaction and he just walked out the door and locked it back.

I got out the chair still holding KJ to walk in the room to see Kyle sitting on the bed next to Amy she was hooked up to an IV it was comforting to know that love out there existed I never been the in love type but looking at them somewhere deep down made me want that.

"Hey Kyle how is she?"

I could see he didn't want to break down he just held her hand tight and continued to stare at her but he never turned my way like taking his eyes off her he would miss something.

"Pa said give her time she should be okay. Do you mind looking after KJ I just want all my attention on her?"

"No I don't mind. I guess."

So I just turned and went in my room holding tight lil KJ. Pa said this, Pa said that. Does anyone here have and original thought? I know they have to obey him to stay alive but I know he just wants to scream right now. I don't blame him for not wanting to be around KJ it just must be too hard but looking down at him would just make your heart melt.

So he finished the bottle and I did an attempt at burping him and cuddled up in the bed maybe in the morning Amy would be better because I'm just not the mothering type.

Chapter 6

What's their story?

I woke up to crying, it was still pitch black for a minute I forgot what was going on. I was having a great dream about being at home.

I felt a sense of loneliness, I never been so alone, so scared. I am the kind of person always in control, not letting no one, or nothing break me down, but here I am having dreams of being home like its right in my grasp.

"Shh...shh...KJ"

I can't believe I fell asleep on the little one, gosh I feel like a complete idiot. I picked up KJ and notice he was wet. I guess I will get my first lesson in diapering so I go across the hall into Kyle and Amy's room to try and find a diaper when I see Kyle slumped over sleep in the chair next to Amy I guess sitting up got uncomfortable. I must have startled him because he jumped up.

"Amy?"

"No Kyle it's me. Where are KJ's diapers and wipes? I'm totally clueless."

I guess it kind of perked him up because he walked over to me and put his arms out for me to hand him KJ; he starred at the little green eyed baby and shed a tear.

"Wow he looks a lot like Amy," he sighed.

"I know I noticed that to, even at only hours old."

He looked up and went blank like I said something wrong.

"Yeah well let me show you some things newbie," We both laughed at that.

No…I'm turning into one of them. We walked over to the crib, that turned into a changing table and he placed KJ down.

"Hold on to him lesson 1: Never leave a baby un-attendant."

"Okay!" I said eagerly like I wanted to learn.

So I placed my hands on his little stomach while Kyle walked over to their closet and opened it to reveal stacks and stacks of diapers as well as totes full of baby clothes. So he grabbed something for him to wear as well as diapers and wipes and walked back over to me but not before giving Amy a quick glance.

Since KJ only had a diaper on, Kyle showed me how to care for the umbilical-cord, and how to put on his clothes and diaper without hurting his frail body.

"Even though he seems frail, you can move his arms and legs around and won't hurt him, just don't move to hard," Kyle explained.

How did he know all these things? It was like he had kids already, he did everything with such an ease about it.

So once he changed KJ and started off putting on the onesie, he let me finish doing the rest.

It was something about him and Pa letting me take over that had me worried, when a baby comes in the picture everyone is one big happy family and that scared me.

I put the little guy's socks on, it was hard because his little feet kept moving around, but I finally slipped the last one on. I picked him up and looked at him like he was a finished project I was proud of.

I hadn't noticed Kyle went back over to the bed and sat back down next to Amy, stroking her face, and moving her bright red hair out of it.

What happen to them? How did they end up here? And the scariest question of all, how long have they been here?

I was heading back out the room when Kyle stopped me. "It's okay Stacy I can take over from here."

In some weird way I didn't want to let him go, it was his father after all but in an instant I had a bond with this little human like I never had with no one else.

"You sure, it's really no problem."

"You did a wonderful job with him, go get some rest."

I reluctantly handed him KJ, and in some way felt an empty hole once I walked away into my room.

I sat back on the bed finding it hard to fall back to sleep, thoughts of grandma entered my head, knowing she must be sick with worry. *Now you care about her being worried Stacy.*

I tried my hardest not to cry about the whole situation, but I felt the Stacy I knew was disappearing, and this scared little girl I once was coming out to play. Not on my watch.

I got up off the bed to look out the window, the moon, and the stars shined bright in the dark sky. I never notice before that they did shine bright; I wasn't slow so that meant we were in some kind of secluded area with no street lights or businesses so we must be far from people.

I tried to focus my eyes and look outside to see again if anything was familiar, but in the dark it was just too hard. I will try again in the morning I know if Kyle, Amy, and I try we will be able to defeat this now that KJ was here.

I sat down on the bed feeling a little defeated but relieved, and slowly laid down, and drifted off to sleep.

I woke up to muffled crying sounds, so I jump out of bed, thoughts of KJ rushed to me.

I ran into the room to find Amy upright in bed trying to breast feed KJ who was against her breast crying.

"Hello stranger, you gave us quite a scare," I interrupted her concentration.

I hadn't notice Kyle wasn't in the room until he came up from behind me with some breakfast in tow.

She looked up and smiled at both of us.

"I heard you were the hero last night," She directed the question at me.

"I just couldn't leave the little guy all alone."

"Well Stacy is a natural," Kyle interrupted while he was setting Amy's breakfast down on a TV tray.

"I wouldn't say that but I did have fun with him as well as I learned something new."

I walked over to the bed and sat down at the edge. Once Kyle had everything ready he took KJ out Amy's arms and handed him to me.

"You have to eat Amy, you have been out for almost a whole day, and after childbirth at that," He lectured her.

Although Amy didn't complain she just did as she was told, but she looked over to me.

"You don't mind, Do you Stacy?"

I looked at her puzzled.

"Mind what?"

"Holding KJ," she said while lifting him out her arms into mine.

"Absolutely not, I think I love this baby more than you two."

I sat there for a minute watching Kyle pick up the room, and Amy eat her food; looking at them everything seemed normal. It didn't seem like we were locked up here, they seemed happy.

So I had to know, I'm sure he wouldn't mind me asking.

"How did you guys meet? Wait first off how did you get here, and how long have you been here?"

Amy almost choked out her food, and Kyle froze in his place. Damn it must be a story behind this...

Chapter 7

A Familiar Face

I sat there and starred at both of them, but they were staring at each other, this intrigued me. Then Amy cleared her throat.

"First off we knew each other before we got here. Kyle was working at this fast food joint I came in to almost every day; I had to admit I had a crush on him."

Kyle expression was one of love when Amy started to explain.

"I also had a crush on her."

Then Amy smiled at him and continued.

"Well like I said before I wasn't the best company to be around, I disrespected my mom everyday; came in the house when I felt like it, grades were a mess at school, and all I cared about was boys."

Sounds very familiar; Who can blame me though it's a typical teenager's life.

It was me all over. Everything she said, she did, I did on a regular basis, I guess you don't appreciate what you have till it's gone, or you're gone.

"Two years ago I was a typical teenager in high school partying like it was my last day on earth; When one late night I was drunk out my body coming from some friends house party when I woke up here."

"So you guys weren't dating?"

Amy continued. "No just harmless flirting he was a goody, goody in my eyes."

So that does explain a lot he stalks us until he finds out our behaviors, our routines, everything about us and we never once suspect it, because we are too busy with ourselves.

"So then Kyle, how did you get here?"

Kyle's eyes went wide with panic, maybe his was worse of a story but Amy interrupted before he could continue.

"Well I was here for maybe a month or two before Kyle even came along, I was here with another couple who just became parents just like us, and I just like you delivered a baby."

My chest grew hollow, my breathe almost gave out, I was still holding KJ so Kyle grabbed him out of my arms, because it did seem like I was going to drop him. I was having a panic attack. Did he expect me to just lie down with someone? No it can't be. I won't let him. Who the fuck does he think he is planning my life out for me no one does that.

"So…you mean…to tell me…," I couldn't even get the words out I don't even know what to say. What the hell was going on? When I thought I knew I would be okay, now my world has come crashing down.

Amy tried to move over to calm me but I could tell she was still in some pain.

"Look Stacy things will be okay, what we found out, is Pa has a different plan for everyone this may not be yours."

I could just smack her, one minute she reminds me cf myself, and the next she is some kind of freak, I will never bow down. They thought they had me falling for this bull. I could see they knew I was mad because Kyle backed away with KJ in his hands, while Amy sat back to the pillows that were propping her up.

"Don't prove him right Stacy, you can change, you can become something better."

I looked at her and nearly spit in her face, just a second ago they had me wanting what they had feeling sorry for them, now the only person I feel sorry for is KJ.

"What the hell makes you think I want to change, I love myself just the way I am," My breathing clear and in control now.

"Don't do this Stacy," Now Kyle spoke up.

"Why? What is he going to do beat me to death?"

I could see their expression on their face, yeah I was talking reckless, but I was mad, I was worse than mad, I was pissed. I balled my fist up got up off their bed and yelled at the top of my lungs.

"NO ONE IS GOING TO CHANGE ME I RATHER DIE"

"Then you shall," Amy spoke softly.

"Remember when I told you about the others, well before you, there were three more, three more like us and three more graves in Pa's backyard"

My now so kill me attitude had been tested. I didn't feel much taller now, now that the truth was out there.

"Let me show you something before you go off," Kyle walked up to me reluctantly grabbed my hand and leaded me to the only window in their room.

I was scared out my mind what he about to show me, but he pulled back the curtain to reveal two other little trailers probably like the one we were in, they were spread over the property but far enough that passerby's wouldn't even notice. I gasped.

I walked back over to the bed and sat down feeling a sense of defeat, he must have been doing this for years and never getting caught every bone in my body wanted to give up and just die, but then my heart said live.

"I understand now, I will….."

But before I could finish my sentence we heard a lot of commotion coming from the front door. I was scared to see Pa coming in I didn't want to leave the safety of the room. What if he heard me? Maybe he was here to finish me off for disobeying.

Then I heard a familiar voice.

"What the hell do you want, you freak."

"Freak, I thought you were a good boy."

I ran in the front entrance to see Trey being thrown on the floor by Pa.

"You respect your elders boy or else."

"Or else what, you can't do nothing to me old man."

I never seen Trey like this, but what would you expect when someone is kidnapping you of course you wouldn't be nice.

Although he didn't know what Pa could do to him?

"I will show you an old man," Pa laughed wildly at him.

He started kicking Trey so hard, blood started shooting out his mouth, I screamed.

"Pa, please no!"

I think that's when Trey noticed I was standing there, so it caught him off guard, "Ace?"

That's when Pa kicked him right in the face. He knocked him right out.

I wanted to run over to him but Pa was standing over him and I was scared out my mind.

"Don't move I will be right back."

By then Amy and Kyle were standing behind me. Pa left out the door and I ran over to Trey shaking him by his shoulders trying to wake him.

"Trey, get up please!"

He started moaning a little bit, but was still passed out. It seemed like only seconds passed when the door flew open again and it was Pa holding a few bags in his hands, he threw them to the floor next to us.

"Since you're here for the long haul you can stop wearing Amy's things."

It was a bag of clothes, now deep down I knew I was his, I belonged to Pa. I was slowly becoming Amy and all the other girls who stay in the other trailers.

Pa walked past us over to Amy and Kyle and picked up KJ out of Kyle's arms, he played with the little guy like nothing happened, like he didn't just kidnap someone and knock them out.

I stared at Pa who was a very tall man he even towers over Kyle, so I knew he had him by a couple of inches, it might sound weird but he was handsome, but in a grandpa sort of way, his smile was wicked, he had dark brown eyes, brown hair cut low to his head, lightly browned skin, and even though he was tall he wasn't fat, he was muscular, but I guess you had to be when you kidnapped for a living you had to be able to overpower your victims.

I looked back down at Trey he was starting to come to, my heart nearly skipped a beat looking at him, I remembered how I lusted over him, that smile he had, and the way he treated me all came crashing back.

"Ace, what are you doing here? The world has been looking for you?"

Of course, Pa must have bashed his head harder than I thought.

"I'm fine are you okay?" I'm slowly sitting him up against the wall.

41

I guess everything started coming into view because he looked over at Pa and started shouting at him.

"Oh you, what the hell is going on here?"

I tried to quiet him but Trey could be very aggressive, although I like it.

Pa started walking towards him, but I stayed in the front of him, I was scared for him.

"Pa, he doesn't know any better please, I will talk to him."

Then Pa smiled at me. "I love this new Stacy; it makes all my hard work even more rewarding."

Now Trey is starting to get up off the ground. "What did you do to her, you bastard?

"Watch your tongue boy, now this here is your new family, ya'll welcome him."

Pa just walked to the door without a shutter, like nothing scared him, he turned and said.

"The ceremony will be held tomorrow, so now you will take your husband, because my family isn't complete yet, I need a lot more of them little guys around."

Chapter 8

Married?

The door slammed like thunder hit. I was shocked what the hell was he talking about husband. I looked at Trey who was still standing up but holding on to his ribs, I think Pa might have broken one, then I looked over at Kyle and Amy their expression wasn't one of shock but one of (hey we knew this was coming.)

I was starting to walk over to them when Trey grabbed my arm with his free hand.

"I was so worried about you. Are you okay? He didn't hurt you did he?"

The questions were oozing out of him; he was concerned about me what about what he just said to us.

"I'm fine Trey, I managed to stay alive, but how in the world did he get you?"

His face started to scrunch up in pain so I helped him over to the dinette set to sit down. Kyle and Amy still stood in the door way but this was more important besides I was indeed angry with them.

He looked at me and started stroking my face, I felt kind of embarrassed, I felt like this should have been a private moment between us, so I looked back over to the doorway and Amy and Kyle were gone.

"Please tell me what happened to you?" I scolded.

"I was leaving the shop again late but instead of going home I was posting missing pictures of you around town. The police seem to think you were a runaway, and you grandmother is worried sick."

"You've seen my grandma?"

"Yes, it wasn't until after the first week you went missing that they finally labeled you as a missing person, but still think you're a runaway, so there not putting much effort into your abduction."

I knew it would turn out this way, the trouble I had been in over the years, they just think I'm a normal misbehaved child who wasn't getting her way at home and went out on her own.

"I was on my way back to my car when a guy came up to me; he asked me if my name was Trey. I thought he was weird so I shrugged him off and told him to get lost. The next thing I know I feel something hard hit me and I'm getting tossed in here."

"You are big and tall why didn't you try to fend him off?"

"Well it could have been the blow to the head," He said sarcastically.

I pulled up his shirt to look at the damage it was starting to swell so I grabbed so ice out of the fridge and wrapped it up in a nearby kitchen towel.

"I need to fix up your head it's still bleeding; it's stuff in the bathroom back here."

So I led him to the bathroom, pulled his shirt over his head. I wrapped up his chest with some elasticized bandage the best way I could, and cleaned up his head wound. It wasn't too bad so all I did was apply some peroxide with some gauze to apply pressure.

"Who were those other people in there?"

Trey caught me off guard while I was fixing him up.

"They are kidnapped victims like us," My voice is in a whisper.

"Why is he holding us here? What did he mean by husband? Ace what's going on in here?"

He had just as many questions as I did when I got here and I'm just now getting my answers. How am I going to tell him he plans on marrying us off and making us produce him some non- related grandkids.

"Well I know why he took me, but…well now I know why he took you. He watches us, stalks us, and preys on us, we are the bad children in his sights, and well at least the girls are, his mission is to reform us, so we won't turn out bad."

"But what does getting married have to do with anything?"

I almost jumped out my skin when Amy and Kyle walked in the room, standing in the door of the bathroom.

"It happened to us, once you learn your lesson he pairs us, and marries us off, but he does it with someone he knows you will be comfortable with, maybe not someone you were dating but someone he knows you're attracted to," Kyle explains.

"Why?" I ask.

"Because like he said before Stacy, he wants more grandkids," Amy explains.

I started to cry I don't want to become a wife or even a mother, I mean I like Trey he's nice, sweet, loving and compassionate, but I'm not the stay at home type and besides how long has this been in the works I've only known Trey since summer started.

Trey gets up and hugs me, *I could get used to this.* The smell of his cologne instantly had my heart skipping a beat, and my lady parts fluttering, his warmth is something I haven't felt in a while and in that moment I felt safer that I have felt in weeks.

I didn't want the hug to end but Trey walked out the bathroom passed Kyle and Amy to look around, he went straight to the windows, but of course they had bars and weren't made of glass, then he left the room and we followed, he went from exit to exit, then he went to Kyle's and Amy's room and again nothing but he did notice the other homes.

"So you mean to tell me there is no way out? Surely we two men can overpower him, His question directed at Kyle.

That was a good idea, but I'm sure Pa wouldn't put two men together if he didn't think he could handle them but hey I wouldn't hurt to try.

"I think that's a great idea," I replied loudly.

"Did you forget he's listening?"

Oh snap I did!

"Oh so the kidnapping bastard can hear us well maybe he can hear this. I will get you, you crazy son of a bitch if it's the last thing I do!"

"He's not stupid you know," Amy's soft voice came in.

"We will starve then, he will not put his self in any danger by coming in here so in turn he will let us starve to death, and that means KJ. You can't let this happen. Stacy!"

"So what do you expect her to do, let the crazy freak to have his way, marry us off and have babies and live trapped ever after? You're just as crazy as he is."

"I can accept your anger but, you need to watch how you talk to my wife, we are in the same boat as you, and we didn't just give up we fought, but we have a son to look after now and we rather survive."

That was the first time I saw Kyle go off like that but his love for Amy is strong and he is passionate about her and he's right they are in the same boat as us, we didn't ask for this but he is right we have to survive.

Trey walked away into the room. I looked up at Kyle and Amy to give them an assuring smile to ease them then followed behind Trey who was already sitting on the bed with his head in his hands.

"Believe me when I say I know what you're going through but it's just not us in here Trey, we have to think about KJ"

I know I could believe it either, me Stacy caring about someone else.

He lifted his head out his hands and smiled at me.

"What?"

"I just can't believe what I'm hearing, not trying to be mean or nothing but this is Ace right?"

"Ha Ha Trey, I just had a long time to think, as well as a good ass whooping to realize the world doesn't revolves around me."

He slide back against the headboard of the bed wincing in pain a little and put his arms out for me. I climbed in and nestle up against him not to close it didn't want to hurt him, but he pulled me in any way's.

"I'm sorry for the way I acted Ace it isn't those people's fault or that little baby, but I just can't see the right in it all. What about you?"

A month ago if he wouldn't asked me this I would had the F it attitude but today I have seen, and experienced a lot of things and you don't have control over everything like you would want to in life.

"I guess it's still wrong, but I know where they are coming from, the just want to survive, and so do I."

I wasn't looking in his face but I could swear he smiled.

Chapter 9

I found a true friend in you

I woke up to the sun shining in my eyes. I felt around the bed no Trey; I jumped up in a panic. Oh maybe Pa decided he wasn't worth the effort. I walked towards the entrance of the bedroom to hear whispering, men voices. I walked towards the kitchen to see Kyle and Trey a lot more chummy than they were last night, but still a relief.

"Hello; am I interrupting something?" I ask.

Both men look back at me with a suspicious look on their face.

"Good morning Ace; I trust you slept well?" Trey announces.

"Like I said before, am I interrupting something?"

"No Ace, I just was apologizing to Kyle for the way I spoke to him and Amy last night. I got a chance to talk to him and understand what's going on."

"Good, I thought you two were concocting an escape plan."

Even though their faces were down because they were preparing breakfast, their eyes still glanced at each other and that had me worried.

Trey walked over to the table with breakfast in his hands and gestured for me to take a seat, he even sat the food down to pull my chair out. *Such a gentleman he is.*

Gosh the food smelled wonderful. They prepared pancakes, bacon, sausages, and eggs. It was so much food you would have thought we were celebrating something instead of being held captive.

Kyle walked Amy's plate into their room while Trey sat across from me at the dinette set.

48

"I'm glad to see you calmed down a bit. I mumbled through chews.

"Oh I forgot your drinks," He said.

He got up from the table to retrieve the already poured milk and orange juice on the counter and handed them to me.

"Yeah I just don't want to risk the safety of you so I will follow your lead but it still doesn't mean I won't take the chance when I see fit; As long as you are safe of course.

I looked Trey in his deep brown eyes, while also scanning the rest of his body, he was handsome as well as a gentleman, I was lucky to be here with him even under the circumstances.

"So what's the deal with this Pa?" he asked.

"Well as far as what I've encountered and been told he has a respect issue and obviously doesn't keep up with the times, he expects women to be obedient and baby making factories. I guess he can't accept that women have a mind of their own now."

It was true somewhere down the line; he must have gotten reality distorted from fantasy. Maybe it was the way he was raised but I'm scared to think what would happen to Trey, he's a nice guy and he's here because I couldn't mind authority. He's here because of me.

"Sorry," I whispered.

"Sorry for what?" His expression was serious.

"Getting you into this mess," I mumble.

"This isn't your fault Ace. Just because someone else's values were distilled upon you, doesn't make you the fall guy."

"I just can't help but to think if we never met, or never flirted," My face flushes after saying that. "He wouldn't have picked you."

Tears were starting to swell up in my eyes. Why was this so hard? I know I wasn't to blame but something in me went out to Trey, maybe because he was such a good guy and I didn't deserve him.

He got up out his seat and crouched down beside me, wiping my tears, and assuring me this wasn't my fault.

"Eat up Ace you need to keep up your strength, we have to stick together."

His words sent shivers down my spine. No man as ever been this willing to stick by me, they all wanted one thing to get into my pants, and I was more than willing to permit it.

I finished my food up and Trey took down a few bites of his. I wasn't that early in the morning maybe around 10am ish. Pa doesn't keep a clock around but I got a glance at Trey's watch earlier.

"Hey Trey I lost track of time. Do know what day and month it is?"

I know it was a silly thing to ask but after a few days I just stop counting.

"It's October 2nd ...Oh wait no 3rd because I have been here over night, it's a new day."

"What I have been here for three weeks, and he has me breaking down like this."

I knew it had been a few weeks but already were in a new month. I was scared how long was he planning on keeping us and did he really expect Trey to marry me?

"I think I'm going to take a shower, I feeling a little flushed."

"Do you need some help?" Trey said while smirking at me.

"No I can manage."

So I headed for the room, while Trey finished up in the kitchen.

I grabbed some clothes out one of the bags that Pa brought me and went in the bathroom. I walked into the bathroom and glanced into the mirror, I don't even recognize myself anymore, I was used to seeing my hair curled up, my face perfectly made up with blush, eye shadow, and to top it off my lip gloss shining. Right now I'm plain.

I turn on the shower and let it heat up and go back to looking at myself.

"You look fine," Smiling admiringly.

I hadn't even noticed Trey looking at me through the doorway. I have to get used to closing the door from now on.

"Really Trey, I look so plain Jane and you know it," I sighed.

"Natural beauty is a woman's perfect weapon, if you can look that good while not having on any make up.....well just say I'd marry you."

"Be serious now, you know if the first time you seen me I looked like this, you wouldn't have even looked twice." I mumble.

"I am being serious, I was always raised to see a woman's inner beauty not all that guck she puts on or the way she dresses; beauty is skin deep."

I know I had to seem so veil to Trey but I always relied on my looks and being in a house with a man that I deeply am attracted to made me feel unattractive looking like this.

The bathroom started to steam up physically, and literally.

"Well thanks for making me feel special," I whispered.

Then he moved out the doorway and closed the door behind him and I proceeded in finishing up my shower.

I wasn't in the shower no more than five minutes when I started to feel dizzy, nausea started to kick in, I washed up quickly, and turned off the shower. I almost lost my footing stepping out the shower, so I set down on the toilet for a minute with the towel wrapped around me, trying to stop the dizziness but it just got worse.

"Trey, can you please….." I hit the ground.

I started vaguely hearing voices whispering was I dreaming?

"You should have stopped her from taking a shower."

"Really what was I going to say, I drugged you so now you need to lay down before you faint."

"Just put her in the bed so I can give her the damn fertility shot."

Chapter 10

Miss Bellows aka Mrs. Collins

I woke up to an aching body I was laying in the bed with pajamas on. What the heck happened? I don't even remember falling asleep.

"Trey, Trey!" I start yelling.

I know he would remember he came running in the room.

"You okay?" Sounding worried.

"What the heck happened I don't even remember falling asleep?"

"You were feeling weak so I helped you out the bathroom and into some night clothes."

I know my face started turning red; he saw me naked!

"Gosh I had the weirdest dream, but just can't remember it; I know it will come back to me."

"Don't bother yourself with that. Do you need help out the bed?"

I tried to move but my body felt heavy, weak, so Trey helped me lift my body to the edge.

"Thanks, I don't know what I would do without you."

He sat down on the bed next to me stroking my leg. I just couldn't believe how lucky I was; when we're out this mess I hope we can continue this romance.

"How long was I out?" I asked.

He looked down at his watch.

"It's just after 12."

"When did Pa say he would be here," I said in a panic.

"I'm not sure, but I can't wait to see that Freak," I could hear the anger in his voice.

"Could you help me up I want to see little KJ."

I missed the little guy even though it's only been a day. So Trey got me off the bed and steadied me to across the hall. We knocked on the door and Amy happily opened.

"Oh gosh Trey should you even have her up after her accident?" She scolded.

"I wasn't even going to argue with her she wanted to see KJ," He said.

"Well we know who the godmother is," She giggled

It caught me off guard godmother to be responsible for a little one was a great responsibility but I wouldn't want anything more that little guy grew on me.

We were still standing in the door entrance when Kyle yelled over.

"Why don't we all go sit in the living space, we never put it to any use, these rooms are starting to get stuffy."

It was a great idea, we never went in there because we were all scared of Pa and it's the first room, when you walk in and no one wanted to be close to him, he still scared the piss out of me even when I did nothing wrong you never know what a man like that is capable of.

Trey helped me over to the smaller couch to sit down, while Kyle and Amy sat on the big one, I'm glad we sat down first because the smaller couch points right to the front door so we would be able to hear and see Pa when he came in. Trey got up off the couch once I was comfortable and handed me KJ while sitting back down with us. He was wrapped up in a blanket so soft and plush, but I had to unwrap it to take a look at his tiny little body then wrapped him back up tight. I held him close for it seemed like hours while I, Trey, Amy and Kyle talked like we were old friends. Everything for the moment seemed normal like we could just open the front door and go home.

Then the door jingled. I knew it was him I could hear all the keys he had probably to all the different trailers that sat in a row behind us. I wondered who Pa really was, was he rich, did he have kids of his own or he couldn't that's why we were caught up in his sick game. I shivered to think of all the answers, but it did bring comfort to me to have Trey right there watching me making sure I was safe.

"It's so good to see all my children mingling with each other," His voice raspy and cold.

I shifted closer to Trey my body stiffened up, the voice scared me, everything about him had me frightened, he valued life, but then had no value for life, he could help bring children into the world but in an instant take someone's life if they didn't obey him and in my eyes he was deranged and cruel.

Trey jumped out his seat, with a cold look in his eye.

"Just let everyone in here go and no one will tell we promise," His voice firm.

"I take it your some kind of hero then? Ok I have a proposition then. You stand here, and she stand there say I do or…… I shoot you both in the head."

Everyone got up Amy quickly moved over to grab KJ and she and Kyle stood behind the small couch, while Trey moved in front of me. Pa still stood at the main entrance waiting for our move.

Then he took out a piece of paper with one hand and lifted his shirt with the other to reveal the gun nestled in his waist. I started to weep was he really going to kill us if we refused but we might as well it's not like it's real or anything you have to legally get married.

I tugged on the back of Trey's shirt to get his attention which was locked square on Pa.

"Let's just get it over with, it's not like its real, just say I do and he will leave us alone," I said in a whisper.

"If we agree to this marriage you won't hurt us right," Trey blurted out.

Pa shook his head with a crazy smile on his face. Trey grabbed my hand and Pa walked closer to us, then passed us into the dining area and placed the piece of paper he had in his hand on the table. With me close to him we walked over to the table to look at what was a marriage license with both our names and Kyle's and Amy's as witnesses. This can't be real can it?

"What's the meaning of this?" Trey spoke sternly.

"This is you guy's marriage license you didn't think I wouldn't do it right did you? So sign now!"

I looked at Trey, he looked at me and we immediately grabbed a pen from out a nearby drawer and jotted down our signature.

Pa pulled out his gun, then a small book out his pocket and started reciting: "Dearly beloved we are gather here today in the sight of God to celebrate the joining of this man and this woman in holy matrimony."

The words started to blur together I stopped listening I started to think about my life at home my mom, the day I found her laid out in her bed with the needle still in her arm. I was only nine years old walking into the bedroom looking into those dead eyes with her pupils small and dilated, her body cold because I ran over to her to try and help her up; you would think a child would block it out but the memory is sealed in my mind for the rest of my life. Grandma had been taking care of me any ways so the courts had no problem giving her custody of me.

Trey's sweating palm on the small of my back snapped me back to reality.

"Stacy Do you pledge to give yourself to Trey freely, comforting and embracing him with intimacy and faithfulness? Do you promise to love, honor, and respect him in good, and bad times, and in sickness, and in health, in plenty, and poverty for as long as you both shall live? Do you take Trey to be your lawfully wedded husband?

I glanced at the gun. "I do," I said slowly.

"Trey, do you promise to provide for Stacy in sickness and in health in good times and in bad times? Do you pledge to protect her from all threats and dangers both from the outside world and within your home? Do you promise to love, honor, and respect her for as long as you both shall live? Do you take Stacy to be your lawfully wedded wife?

"I do," he said.

"With the power invested in me I now pronounce you husband and wife, you may now take your bride. Now kiss!"

Trey pulled me in closer and planted the softest kiss on my lips, tears started to stream down my face I tried my hardest not to cry but I felt like my life wasn't my own anymore.

"You shouldn't be crying this is your wedding day," Pa replied.

"These are tears of joy," Trey replied sarcastically.

"Well great! Kyle, Amy I need your John Hancock and I will be out of you love birds way," He giggled.

The world seemed blurry to me, my face was so wet and I felt dizzy from crying I didn't know what to do, was this marriage really real? It was a real marriage license wasn't it? I'm so confused.

"Now I would appreciate if you start right away making my grandkids; it took Amy and Kyle a year to conceive I don't have time like that."

"What?" I choked out.

"Amy, Kyle finish up here I don't have time to get violent in front of the child, well not unless you want me to?

Kyle walked closer to Pa like he wasn't scared at all.

"Look Pa we will explain everything, you can leave because your presence only makes Stacy scared and pisses Trey off more we have it under control."

He just collected his paper and walked to the door. Then I snapped.

"It's one thing to play your game about being fake married but you will not force me to lay down with him, I don't even know him like that and I'm definitely not having anyone's baby's."

Pa face turned pale all the joy drained out of it; it went so cold I regret saying what I said in an instance. He started walking back over to me but Trey jumped in his way trying to fight the gun out his hand.

"No, I'm sorry; please don't hurt him I will do whatever you tell me we will make your baby."

It was too late. Pa over powered Trey threw him against the wall. POW!

Chapter 11

Amy POV/ Things are not as they seem

Why does everything around here feel like déjà vue? Is this what he does to everyone if they don't comply? Something doesn't set right with me I will have to pull Stacy to the side to talk to her later but how? He's always listening. *Oh wait I never thought about writing it down yeah that will work.*

"By the way everything about that marriage was real; like I said before I have a lot of things covered I went to school for a lot of things to keep my family as I want, so if he means something, anything to you nurse him to health," Pa said calm and coldly.

Pa left Stacy there in shock staring at a bleeding Trey; we weren't exactly sure where he shot him until Kyle picked him off the ground to help him in the shared bathroom we have.

Still Stacy stood there in shock I guess everything was more than she could handle. I remember it like it was yesterday, standing in the same spot she was standing in watching Kyle laid there on the floor, although Pa stabbed him. Kyle was always a gentleman but it's a lot to take in when a man tells you to marry a relatively stranger as well as produce babies it was more than him or I could take and he snapped.

I had been in here with Ethan and Harper for three months before she had her daughter and she was too sweet and welcoming as I have been to everyone since her. I never knew what became of her she left here the same day she had…what was it? Oh Amanda. Such a beautiful baby she was, she had the most beautiful hazel eyes, soft brown hair, it covered her entire head, and smooth brown skin.

It was something about girls Pa didn't like, I could hear them arguing about her and her turning out like these whores now and days. I hope nothing happened to them because they were the reason I fell in love with Kyle. Watching them and seeing how they made it gave me hope and made me realize Kyle was my knight in shining armor as well as my one true love.

Kyle and I lived here for months with me nursing him to health and watching Pa bring in girl after girl they weren't obedient at all , it was far too murders than I would have liked to see in my whole life.

I remember one in particular her name was Kailani she was of African American and Hawaii descent, she was very beautiful but she couldn't be broken, Pa beat her for days straight before he thought she wasn't worth his time and disposed of her and he made me and Kyle watch and her murder haunts me more than the rest, that's why I'm going to do everything in my power not to see that happen to Stacy, I will teach her.

"Stacy! Snap out of it," I shout.

I didn't want to frighten her but she had to help us with Trey.

"Amy, go put KJ down in his crib I need help," Kyle shouts from the bathroom.

I head into the room to set KJ down running to help Kyle, once I put him down I glance back down the hall Stacy is still standing there, I will get to her later.

Kyle already has Trey laying in the bathtub with the shower running on him, he rips his shirt off and we see a small gunshot hole right through the side of his chest. Kyle begins to apply pressure while I grab all the first aid kit supplies, once we stop the bleeding Kyle patches it up the best way he can and carries an unconscious Trey to the bed.

I go back in the living area and Stacy is still in the same spot, it looked like she hadn't blinked in 20 minutes, her eyes were blood shot red and wet with tears. I fill up some water in a cup and throw it on her that's all I could think of to snap her out of it.

"Is he dead?" She mumbles.

"No Stacy, he's resting in the bed, Kyle and I fixed him up but you have to help. I know this is a lot but he's counting on you."

I tried to sound as convincing as I knew how to, I couldn't see any more death not with KJ around I just can't do it or I might break down also. It's hard for us too they all used to think we were crazy but the only crazy thing was mouthing off a lunatic, who knows what he could do to you and after my first beating I knew exactly what he could do, I couldn't walk for a month; Stacy had it easy.

She managed to get herself together and walked back into the room, she stood there and stared at him for a minute then climb up in the bed and carefully snuggles up to him on the other side of his wound.

"It's my fault, so I will do everything I can for you I promise," She whispers in his ear but we still hear her.

"Kyle, Amy. Are we really married? Was he telling the truth?"

It was a good question I always considered Kyle my husband but I wasn't never really sure if it was one of Pa's sick games or was it really legal.

"I don't know Stacy, but with him you never know," I said truthfully.

Stacy laid her head back down and me and Kyle walked out.

"You can go back into the room I will clean everything up," Kyle sighed.

"KJ is sound asleep I won't let you do this alone," While rubbing his back.

It was something in Kyle's face today that was hard for him we used to clean up all the other girls and of course it bothered him but something was different this time and I just didn't feel right leaving the love of my life alone.

"Thanks," he said.

We cleaned up the living room and bathroom and then took a shower and cleaned ourselves off and cooked us something to eat and retired to bed early.

Stacy POV

I lie in the bed next to a motionless Trey all except for his slow and steady breathing, a reminder to me that he's still with me. I glance over at his wound it's starting to seep out so I go into the bathroom to get some more supplies. It's so funny how Pa keeps these bathrooms supplied with equipment he must know to break people he has to give them a good ass whipping. Then I wonder again how long he has been doing this.

I find some more wrapping and some antibiotics and proceed to cleaning the wound. I'm not good at this so Trey wakes up then I notice he's sweating heavily.

"Are you okay?" He asks me.

Priceless, he's the one shot and bleeding out and he asks me am I alright. How did I get so lucky?

"I'm fine. You need to worry about yourself. Why on earth would you attack that crazy ass man? He could have really killed you and I need you. I can't possible survive here without you."

"Don't worry I'm not going anywhere. I'm sorry, I wasn't thinking about me. I was thinking about you and his demands of making you sleep with me. I would never take advantage of you. You know that right? His words sincere.

"I know that but we will eventually have to meet his demands but for now let's get you well," I smiled.

I continued to fix Trey up. It was still early but the sun was started to set.

"Hey do you want something to eat we haven't eaten since breakfast this morning and my stomach is growling," I exclaimed.

He sat up in the bed the best way he could but making faces in the process.

"I'm okay let's just lie back in bed," He said rather excitedly.

"Well if you don't want anything I'm still hungry so I will be back in a second."

I headed in the kitchen despite Trey's eagerness for me to stay in bed with him and searched the cabinets and fridge to find me something to eat. I never notice before but it was tons of gallons of milk and orange juice in there. I wonder if that's their favorite.

Anyways I made me a quick sandwich because that is the only thing that you could make that was quick. I was discarding the empty package that held the lunch meat in it and glanced down, I had to double look. Was that a syringe?

Chapter 12

Wifely Duties

I knew it was stupid to pick it up but, why in the world was there a syringe in the trash? I started to think about the dream I had did Pa drug me again?

Oh God I hope not because who knows what he did to me. I decided not to pick it up. I didn't want to accidentally poke myself just in case it was some type of hardcore drug.

I took my sandwich into the bedroom to see Trey trying to get out of bed.

"What are you doing? Do you want to bleed out?" I blurted out nearly scaring him.

"No. I just don't want you wondering this place alone just in case the freak might come back."

"Trust me, as long as we do what he tells us nothing will happen to us."

I sat at the edge of the bed and ate my sandwich while Trey scooted back to the top of the bed, still wincing in pain.

I finished up my sandwich and scooted in the bed next to him again. I took a double glance at the wound to make sure I didn't need to play doctor again before I really went to sleep.

"I wish I had some pain medicine, this shit really hurts," he said.

"I wonder why he won't give us any pain medicine, He must think we will try to escape that way," I mumbled.

I looked at Trey he was sweating even worse. I hope the wound isn't infected. Why is he torturing us so?

"Do you need me to do anything for you?" I ask him.

He just shakes his head and starts to drift off.

I wake up and the lights are turned on in the room. I start to adjust my eyes and realize Pa is in the room with Kyle.

"What's going on what are you doing to him?" I shriek.

Pa is over Trey who is unconscious with his wound bleeding heavily.

"Patching him up, what else would I be doing?"

Was that a freaking trick question, *uh maybe finishing him off?*

I look over at Trey even though he's unconscious he doesn't look too good. I jump out the bed and head in the bathroom to get a face towel to wet it with cold water. I walk back into the room and start wiping Trey's face with it, he doesn't even flinch.

Pa is cleaning his wound and starting him on an IV like he did Amy, I wonder what changed his mind? I stand next to Kyle who is assisting Pa with patching him up. I know I'm still scared of Pa but I can't help to be grateful that he is helping Trey.

"I'm going to go get some ice," I say.

I head in the kitchen grab a big bowl out the cabinet and drop all the ice in the Trey. I run back into the bed room to see Pa pulling a bullet out Treys chest with some type of forceps, he starts to sew him up then he puts bandages back over the wound, and starts to pack his bag.

"Well all done he should be good as new in a few hours, but make sure you change the bandages frequently so the infection doesn't get worse."

I walk up to Trey and put my hand on his forehead, "So he does have an infection?"

"Yes but you did a great job keeping the wound clean," he says proudly.

That must have been his plan to begin with to see if I'm good wife material for Trey but at the risk of his life?

I'm more determined than ever to get out of here he has to slip up eventually. Once Trey is healthy we will get out I'm sure of it, we just have to play our cards right.

Trey's side of the bed is covered in blood but I dare not wake him so I grab a chair from the other side of the room and pull it close to him. I put some ice in the towel and place it on his forehead. I keep it that way for a while until my arm gets tired and I drift off.

"Ace, Ace wake up," Trey tries to wake me while lightly shaking me.

"What? What time is it? I hadn't even realized I fell asleep."

I looked up to see Trey removing the sheets from the bed, while holding his side with his free hand. I get out the chair and stretch a little because my body is stiff from sleeping in a chair.

I start to grab the rest of the bedding, "What the heck are you doing? If you hadn't realized you were shot yesterday and been bleeding out ever since."

Trey continued to tug with me for hold of the bedding, "I feel fine so let me finish."

I wonder what Pa gave him last night? Besides the obvious wound and the soreness because he still holding his side he looks fine.

"Well, let me at least get Kyle to take the IV out your arm," He's looking down as though he hadn't even noticed it was there.

"Okay," he said sounding annoyed.

I walked across to the room, I was just about to knock when I heard commotion coming from there but it whisper voices.

"I need some paper," An annoyed Amy bustling around. I hear dressers opening and closing.

"Paper, what do you need with paper?" Kyle mumbled.

"Look can you get me some paper or not, he seems to always get you what you want," Her voice sounding suspicious.

I knocked on the door and silence be stilled on the room like I startled them "Kyle, Amy it's me Stacy. I was wondering if Kyle could talk Trey into taking this IV out his arm. The door swung open. Kyle was standing in the doorway.

"No problem," He slid past me and into the room.

So I walked in to find Amy still searching for some paper I guess, but I ignored her and walked to KJ's crib; the little guys lay there sleeping away without a worry in the world.

So I plopped down on the bed, "So what cha doin? I ask her nonchalantly.

"Looking for some paper and something to write with, that's all, got a lot on my mind," she confesses.

Then she stopped in her tracks like something dawned on her, "You want to make a special dinner for the guys tonight?" but before I could answer she mouthed, "We need to talk."

I looked around the room she must need to tell me something about Pa.

"Don't say anything I want it to be a surprise," So what I got from that was, she needed to tell me something but don't tell Kyle or Trey, weird.

"Okay," I answered shrugging my shoulders.

KJ started to cry so Amy went to pick him up. Leaving me an opening to leave, I walk back into the room to catch Kyle and Trey whispering again but all I caught out of it is she getting suspicious. *What the hell?*

I cleared my throat and walked in, "Good to see the IV out, did he put up a fuss?"

"None what's so ever," Kyle said while walking past, "See ya guys later."

I went in the room and sat back in the chair that sat by the bed, "So what were you two conversing about?"

"Nothing," he said while wiping the invisible wrinkles out the bed, "Kyle's just worried about Amy that's all."

"Sure," I said, "So what's on the agenda?" I said while leaning back in the chair, knowing full well we had no plans outside this house.

"I'm beat just making the bed and all," he sighed.

"You're hard headed, didn't I tell you?" I laughed, "Come I will lay with you until you fall asleep for a nap."

So I got out the chair and pulled the sheets back to help him in the bed, I closed the bedroom door and got in bed next to him stroking his chest ,"You feel okay right?"

"Yeah, I'm fine why do you ask?

"I'm just happy to see that you are okay, I was petrified when I woke up and saw Pa standing over you I…. I just thought you were a goner."

I don't want to be alone again now that Trey is here with me. I started to stroke his chest some more , feeling his warmth making me shiver, he put his hand against the arch of my back making my lady parts jump, then he leaned down for a kiss. It was so passionate I didn't want to stop; I think I got a little ruff.

I got on top of him never breaking the kiss, I position my body so I wasn't on top of his wound, he put his hands on my breast causing me to become wet instantly, he broke the kiss to start to suck my breast, I started to move my body stroking up and down.

"Are you sure?" he asked coming up from my breast.

"Yes," I moaned.

I got up and removed my pajama bottoms, then Trey slide his shorts and boxers down his manhood was already standing tall waiting for me, I got back on top of him and he thrust himself in me like he couldn't wait to be inside me his arms tightened around my waist. I thought he would bust a stitch the way he was thrusting me up and down I moaned louder and louder matching his strokes, then our bodies went limp.

I got up and felt a little shame of myself, I mean I'm no virgin but I guess I have more respect for Trey and I don't want him thinking I'm a whore or something.

"You okay?" he said while dressing himself.

"Yeah I'm fine," I lied.

He walked over to me while I was pulling my pajamas back on, "Don't you ever feel like you did something wrong. I have cared about you for so long, before we even got here, so we need to make the best out of this bad situation and besides we're husband and wife," he chuckled.

He was right I had him, and I knew Trey cared about me and I wasn't worried about getting pregnant I mean I was on birth control before I got here I know it didn't dissolve out my body just yet, as long as we were so called trying to do as Pa wished he wouldn't hurt us, Right?

Chapter 13

Not really what I was expecting

After our little talk I felt a little better so I got back in the bed with Trey and we talked for hours until Amy knocked on the door ."Hey Stacy can I talk to you?" she yelled through the door.

I jumped out the bed and went to the door, "hey what's up?" I said eagerly.

She started scratching her head like she was nervous about something, "Remember earlier?" her tone low.

She never gave me any eye contact something is up with her, "Oh yeah, you ready to start now?"

I could hear Trey moving in the bed, "Ace come back to bed."

Never breaking contact with a flustered Amy, "give me a minute go run the shower and I will meet you there." I said trying to distract him.

I closed the door behind us and walked in the kitchen, sitting on the dining room table were some bags of groceries, and personal stuff, "What's all this?" I looked at her puzzled.

"Pa, he comes in once a week to restock the pantries and other things."

Weird I never even heard him come in or anything, I glanced down at the trash it was empty too. Amy started to put the things up still looking towards the back. What's wrong with her?

"You okay Amy?"

She jumped a little, "Oh, yeah… me? I'm fine."

I walked over to her and started to help her unload the groceries, I got through the second bag and seen a notepad, "Hey someone came through for you."

"What?" she turned and looked from over by the cabinets.

She hurried over to me and opened it up, it was a small tablet with a pen attached, and she immediately started writing: **DON'T SLEEP WITH TREY SOMETHING IS GOING ON AND I CANT PUT MY FINGER ON IT.** I Read as she was writing it.

Something is going on? Has she truly lost her marbles? Yeah something is going on we have been held prisoner by a crazy man who wants us to play house. *She has been here far too long.*

I grabbed the pen from her: **WHY? IT DOESN'T MATTER IT'S TOO LATE ANYWAY.**

She was just about to continue writing when both Trey and Kyle came out the room simultaneously, Kyle holding KJ.

Amy ripped the piece of paper off the pad quickly, if you weren't close enough you probably wouldn't even notice, so I know they didn't see, because I turned around and didn't even see where she put the ripped piece of paper.

"You guys are ruining the surprise," Amy walked closer to Kyle, with a much more calm tone, kissing him on the cheek.

I played along. "Yeah we were going to cook you guy's dinner; you are always cooking for us."

They both grinned from ear to ear.

 "Besides you need to sit down before you bust a stitch."

"I was waiting for you in the shower I could have turned into a prune waiting for you," He giggled.

"Well go lay back down, and I will bring you dinner when it's done," I said trying to push him into the room.

"I will just take a seat on the sofa, to keep you company," he said while walking past me into the living room.

"Great idea," Kyle said with enthusiasm while moving in with a sleeping KJ in his arms.

So I guess no more writing in secrecy right now, if I didn't know any better they seemed a bit suspicious.

Amy and I continued to put up the groceries, along with some personals, like soap, pads, deodorant, Pa made sure we were very stocked up. I wonder what the supermarket clerk thinks when he comes to the counter with piles, and piles of female feminine products?

I hadn't really cooked here before so it was difficult to use the plastic stuff to cut up the vegetables with; I don't know how in the world Amy does this.

I guess she seen the difficultly I was having so she pushed me out the way and directed me to boiling the noodles; we were making homemade chicken soup.

"Dinner was great," Kyle bellowed out.

"I second that," Trey said while rubbing his belly.

I guess they didn't want to leave us alone so we ate in the dining area.

Amy got up from the table and started to grab a fussing KJ from out his little bouncy seat.

"I will get him," Kyle said.

She leaned in and kissed him, "Thanks, So Stacy and I can start on cleaning up."

I looked around we already cleaned up before we sat down so I knew that was Amy's code for we still need to talk.

Although reluctant both men exited the room, Amy instantly removed the piece of paper she had out her bra and burned it on the stove. The stench of burned paper filled my nostrils. I guess my face turned up so Amy started to wave her hand to keep the smell from traveling.

She looked around to see if the guys were coming back and started to write again: **DON'T SLEEP WITH HIM AGAIN AND YOU SHOULD BE FINE IT TOOK ME AWHILE TO GET PREGNANT.**

I worded okay and she burned the piece of paper and threw the remainder of it in the sink and ran the water and stuck the note pad in a nearby drawer and we parted ways like nothing was ever said.

I went back into the room to see a smiling Trey in the bed naked, "Ready for round two," he said while moving his eyebrows.

Then his face frowned up, he must have smelled the paper, I hope he doesn't ask any questions.

"Feeling a little tired, I'm going to take a quick shower and call it the night," I said walking toward the bathroom.

His expression changed drastically but I just walked into the bathroom.

I stood in the shower letting the hot water drip off my body thinking about what Amy said I'm not stupid I know you can get pregnant the first time, but like I said I have been on birth control pills for years and I just feel that even if I haven't had them for a month I still could have some effects still in my body.

I shrug it off and finished up the shower.

I dry myself off and put a towel on, when I walk into the room Trey is still lying in the bed looking at the ceiling in the same position that I left him, I didn't want things to be awkward between us so I dressed put on a long t-shirt and cuddled in the bed with him.

"You okay?" he said turning on his side to look in my face.

"Yeah, perfect it's…..just, well …never mind."

He just looked at me never asking me nothing, he's so trusting never questioning me.

I move my body around a little bit and find a comfortable position, his face still right in front of me so I can smell the sweetness of his breathe, warm and welcoming.

Trey grabs my waist bringing me in closer to him making my body shiver, I feel a lump in my throat, and I never felt like this before. *Hey what's the worst that can happen?* I give in to Trey, again.

Time seems to drift slowly through the last few weeks. Amy and I are still tag writing but I couldn't bring myself to tell her I have been still sleeping with Trey. I can't help it, I love him and I know it's real he makes me feel safe and loved ,besides she has been off her rocker, Pa has kept her locked up too long, sometimes I just don't know how to talk to her, it's like walking on egg shells so I know Kyle is having it hard.

Pa hasn't been around a lot just the once a week shopping bags that he has been dropping off, so things seem normal, well normal to be locked away and kidnapped.

Amy and I are in the kitchen unloading the bags of groceries as usual, but I notice Pa has a lot of extra stuff this time, he has some clothes for KJ since he has grown so big in the last few weeks, as well as extra food. I dig through the bag and right at the bottom of the last bag I see 4 pregnancy tests "What the fuck," I yell out.

74

"What?" Amy rushes over to me.

She looks down in the bag, and then at me "What did I tell you Stacy?" she scolded me.

I feel guilty as hell, like my grandma caught me doing something, but the thing is I never really cared about how anyone looked at me, but she just had the worst look in her eyes.

Trey and Kyle run into the kitchen with the wind flying behind them, "What's going on?"

I just stare into the bag, contemplating, I feel completely fine, there's no way I'm pregnant. *What? He knows something I don't.*

Trey walks over to me putting his hand on the small of my back, "What wrong Ace?"

I never looked up from the bag, then a tear slides down my face, and that's when I felt sick.

I run in the shared bathroom and puck out my guts, barely making it to the toilet, I hear footsteps trailing behind me.

"It's okay Ace."

I hear Trey's voice barely recognizable, it's like he's miles away, my eyes are so welled up I can't even see straight, the smell of old eggs from breakfast this morning makes me gag some more.

I get up from the toilet well aware that my breath is riddled with left over puke.

"This can't be, I have been on birth control for years, for the reason I don't want any fucking kids, I can't be pregnant this quick, he did something to me I know it, I've been here for a little over two months there is no way my birth control lost its effect so soon" I start pushing Trey out the way he seems to think he can soothe me, "Pa I know you hear me, what did you do to me?"

"Stacy shut up; do you want him to come in here?" Amy whispers.

Then reality hits me, she is right what is wrong with me? There's a fucking killer out there, I run in the bedroom bathroom and shut the door.

I sit in the bathroom for it seems like hours, everything is quiet, I don't even hear KJ, the silence is eerie, I hear birds outside chirping, never have I heard complete and utter silence. I'm afraid to go outside this bathroom because I know he came in there and killed everyone because he was tired of my smart ass mouth. *Now I'm next and he's just making me sweat.*

I couldn't take the silence any more it's time to meet my maker, I got up off the ground just in time to hear whispers I got knots in the pit of my stomach, I leaned up against the door. *I never said I wouldn't go out fighting.*

"Ace," I hear Trey's voice behind a light knock, "Please open the door we need to talk."

I reluctantly opened the door to see Trey holding all four pregnancy tests in his hand. I knew we had to know for sure but I was scared. I never thought Pa would win, I didn't want to turn out like Amy, crazy as hell, *but I just might.*

I sat down on the toilet not even saying a word to him just held my hand out, and then he sat down on the floor in the doorway. I did the first one POSITIVE, and the second one POSITIVE, I only did the third one because I couldn't believe it; he must have known what he was doing because I hadn't even had my period. It was an early response test and I was indeed pregnant.

Chapter 14

Cliché

I stayed on the toilet crying my heart out, I'm only 17 and now I will become a mother, what a cliché.

Trey gets up off the floor and walks over to me rubbing my back, "I'm sorry."

It's not his fault, it's Pa's fault well not all his fault we did know what we were doing, but it's not like we had a choice, if we didn't we would have been as sure as dead.

I got up off the toilet and walked into the room and sat on the bed and curled into a ball, I didn't want to be touched I didn't want to be talked to, my life has become a nightmare, and I just tried to pretend everything was good. I tried to dilute myself into thinking if I had sex I wouldn't become pregnant, as well as I wasn't really married. This is probably how Amy finally snapped.

"Ace, I promise I will not let anything happen to you and my baby, but you have to promise me something."

I was intrigued by that question, I sat up in the bed wiping away my tears to see what promise Trey wanted me to keep, "Go on," I sniffled.

"No matter what, you will never leave me?"

Why would he think I would leave him? "Trey this is neither mines nor your fault, we were just caught up in this sick game, and for the fact that you have stuck by me, loved me, and took care of me, I will never leave you. I'm not sad that I'm pregnant with your baby, I'm said it happened like this."

Tears were streaming down my face more but it was true I fell in love with Trey and I will never leave him, once we get out of here, we will raise our baby together because I have hope that Pa will indeed slip up one day.

I got out of bed to hug Trey to assure him that I would indeed never leave him when I felt a slight cramp as I got up, which causes me to slightly bend over in pain; Trey immediately grabs me "Ace you okay?"

"Yeah I…think it's just a cramp," I sigh.

"I'm no doctor but since you're pregnant I don't think cramps should occur," he said sounding worried.

"Just help me over to the bed."

He helped me over to the bed and made sure I was comfortable before he went to leave the room, "hey where are you going?"

"I'm going to send Amy in here with you to keep you company while I talk to Kyle," he said while walking out the room.

Only moments passed and Amy came into the room holding a sleeping KJ in her arms, "You okay? Trey sounded worried about the cramp," she said while taking a seat on the bed.

"I'm fine, I only felt it when I stood up but I'm no doctor I wouldn't even know how to take care of myself while I'm pregnant," I sighed.

"Don't feel bad I didn't know the first thing either, but you mothering instincts kick in, just remember how you took care of KJ when I was incapacitated," she said while shaking KJ in her arms.

I did feel a responsibility to the little guy and I know if my bond was strong with him I know I wouldn't have no problem caring for my own child.

Kyle and Trey walked into the room with Pa pushing a big tube like instrument it must be an ultrasound machine, Amy instantly moved from the bed out the way. I flinched as Pa moved closer to me, "We have to make sure the child is okay, cramps are not a good sign in pregnancy," Pa said while setting up the machine.

Trey came over to me and whispered in my ear, "Everything will be okay just let him do what he needs to do for our baby."

I decided not to argue with him, he was right I had to make sure my baby was okay, my first responsibility as a mother to be. Although in the back of my head I wondered how in the hell he got here so fast and knew what was going on.

I lay back in the bed with the help of Trey propping my pillow up to make sure I was comfortable.

"Remove your pants," Pa said with a lot of force.

"What?" Trey yelled.

"Don't get loud with me boy, do as I say."

Why might I ask?" I mumbled out.

Then I hear Amy's voice from across the room "Because you are not far enough along to see the baby on your abdomen on a traditional ultrasound, you have to go in internally its call a Trans-vaginal ultrasound."

Just hearing her explain it to me made me feel better but I don't want him anywhere near my vagina.

"Well do you need me to insert it," Kyle suggested.

"Do you have a medical degree boy?"

You probably don't either.

"No, but it's my wife you're fondling with," Trey became angry.

The word wife caught me off guard, it felt weird but nice.

"I respect the sanctity of marriage, just close your eyes and pretend I'm a doctor at an office," he said calmly.

"We will excuse ourselves," Kyle announced.

Once the two of them were out the room Pa closed the door and Trey helped me remove my pajama pants, and pulled the sheet over me, Trey moved to the top of the bed holding my hand while Pa moved down to the bottom of me pulling the sheet up. I held Trey's hand so tight that I thought maybe I would squeeze all circulation out of it. I shut my eyes tight but it still didn't stop the tears from sliding down them, and then I felt the tube go up me I tensed up quickly "Relax child, I won't do you any harm," he whispered.

Sometimes his voice can be so soothing that I forget where I am then reality hits me hard, I'm married, pregnant and trapped but the squeezing of Trey's hand reminds me that I'm not alone.

Pa starts to move the probe around slightly that it makes me feel violated, maybe if it was a real doctor and not the man who kidnapped me I would handle it better.

"Okay, the picture is becoming clearer ah there it is," Pa let out a sigh of relief.

I opened my eyes to see Trey gazing into the ultrasound machine that's when I say it for myself not quite a baby but a small white circle.

"Well everything seems fine, the yolk sac is attached properly, I don't see a heartbeat quite yet," My heart nearly dropped, "But that only means the fetus is too young to detect, I'm going to say your right around 5 weeks or so."

It hasn't even been a month yet why I am so far along; I will just ask Amy I don't want to be around Pa no more than I have too.

Pa starts to slip the probe back out me making me flinch again, he pulls the condom off it that I hadn't even notice he put on there and balls it up in the rubber gloves he had on, and flings it in the trash can he has attached to the machine.

"Okay do you guys have any questions?" he looks at both of us.

I sit up in the bed and put the sheet back over my bare legs "No I don't, Trey?"

I hadn't even notice Trey was in a daze "Um…no I'm good…well wait, I'm asking you man to man now that Ace is pregnant do you think you can let us go, I don't want being stuck in here stressful on the baby."

Pa looked at Trey like he was considering his proposition.

" I'm thinking your due date is somewhere towards the end of June but I will be back in three weeks for another ultrasound to pin point it correctly," And he just grabbed the machine and started wheeling it out like Trey didn't say nothing to him.

"Don't try shit boy, I'm packing I learned my lesson with you. I will shot her right in the gut first then you in the head so don't try nothing and believe me when I say you are replaceable but I like Ace," he said while glancing back at me which sent shivers down my back.

I knew from Trey body language he wanted to rush him and he probably would of but Pa was smart he walked backwards until he was out of view and walked out the door locking it back as usual.

"I'm done Trey I'm swear on this baby the first chance I get I'm getting the fuck out of here I'm not raising my baby in here," I whispered even though I knew he wasn't back in the house to hear me.

Trey looked at me his eyes watering with tears, "What do you expect me to do you heard him he will kill us baby or not."

This shit is getting to real for me, I will leave it alone and talk to Amy I don't want to worry Trey because he will just worry about the baby.

I lay in the bed and Trey came back into the room with something to drink for me, "Here if you're not going to eat at least drink something."

I took the cup of orange juice gulp it down and laid down I drifted off soon after. I woke up to a dark room and no one in sight, I got up out the bed feeling a little dizzy that I lost my footing I held on too anything I could dragging across the walls until I got to the entrance of the doorway. I thought I heard the door slam.

"Ace, get in the bed you should be resting," Trey's voice came through in a fog.

I tried to adjust my eyes to see I could barely make out his face and a shadow standing behind him, then I felt Trey lift me up cradling me in his arms, he laid me in bed, then I felt a slight pinch in my arm like a mosquito bit me "Trey what's going on.....?"

Chapter 15

Double Trouble

I woke up refreshed but stiff I stretched my body out then swung my legs over the bed because Trey wasn't next to me the room was empty, I headed for the bathroom to refresh myself, not sure what the time…or day was.

"Hey beautiful how are you and my bundle of joy," Trey said smirking in the doorway.

I jumped a little, "Where were you?" I shrieked.

"I was in the kitchen with Kyle making something for our lovely wives to eat," he laughed.

"Nice," I said not looking at him just staring at myself in the mirror; my eyes were puffy and red and seemed to be black circles around them.

"Gosh, I look horrible," I exclaimed.

"Well you did sleep through the night hard," he mumbled.

"Since I have been here I have been having some weird dreams," I said while wiping my face with a cold rag.

"Why kind of dreams" he said moving closer to me in the bathroom.

"I don't know I just had a weird dream about a door slamming," I spaced out thinking about it.

Trey assured me it was just a dream but I definitely wasn't buying it.

"Well don't worry yourself about such things, come to the dining room when you are done freshening up" he laughed walking out the bathroom.

I walked out the bathroom and checked the dresser for something to wear, I found a tank top shirt and some sweat pants which has been my norm lately but not my usual. I miss wearing my tight pants and belly shirts, oh and don't get me started on makeup...the good ole days.

I took off the pajamas that I had on not even remembering when the hell I put them on and noticed my belly ring was sore and my stomach wasn't flat anymore, it wasn't showing tremendously but I definitely knew myself I was pregnant as if I didn't know before, Pa said I was only 5 weeks where the hell did that come from, it kind of looked like I ate too much for dinner. I pulled out the belly ring and set it down on the dresser and finished dressing and walked into the dining area.

"Hey you guys look at my stomach," I lifted my shirt and Amy gasp.

She got up off the table and walked over to me, "That wasn't there yesterday," she said while rubbing my belly.

I thought the same thing. Was I growing some kind of alien baby?

I put my shirt down and walked over to the table.

"Hey Trey by any chance are you some kind of alien? I laughed between chews.

"Ha ha," Maybe you're the alien.

I pushed his shoulder and we continued to eat breakfast.

"Hey Amy I meant to ask you, do you know why I am so far along Pa said 5 weeks," I asked.

She stopped chewing on her food and looked up at me, "I know I wondered the same thing, they go by your last period to figure in the due date, it's different than, the actual conception date"

I started to laugh then everyone looked at me, "What?" I said.

"I felt the same way too," Amy giggled.

Both men looked at us but she knew what I meant we didn't know shit about being a mother but everything is a lesson learned.

"But I have a book you can read, that's how I learned what I needed to know," Amy said.

I was getting up from the table," Hey Ace, don't forget your orange juice."

I made a gagging noise, "No way I'm drinking that I'm so tired of orange juice you drink it, and I don't think it agrees with the little alien," I said while patting my belly.

"But you need it for vitamins and stuff," he said.

"Well I rather eat a pill than drink another glass of orange juice, I noticed that the only dang thing in here besides milk and water is orange juice, he does know there are other liquids in the world right?"

Amy and I busted out laughing but it didn't seem all that funny to Trey and Kyle they just traded looks to one another.

"Well just drink it one last time for me and when Pa comes for his grocery drop off I will try to convince him to get something else, okay?"

"Well if it means that damn much to you," And I grabbed the cup and gulped it down gagging while it was going down, "There I'm done with orange juice," And I slammed the cup on the table and went into the room.

I curled right back into the bed because my body was still stiff and I was tired as hell, I was tired of this life boring and tiresome but I can't do anything until me and Amy are alone and have a great plan.

"You okay Ace?" Trey said standing in the doorway smiling.

"No, I'm sick of this life and this everyday bull crap, I need to get some air or I will snap," I yelled but not too loud.

"All you need to do is stay safe and carry that baby to the best of your abilities and I will do the rest," he said while walking to the edge of the bed.

"Sure," I exclaimed, "can we not talk about this I'm really tired," I said while drifting off quickly.

The dreams I have been having scare me I feel like reality is fooling me, sometimes I wonder am I really even here or am I just dreaming it.

I sit up in the bed looking down at my stomach the month has gone by so quickly, Amy says I'm almost out my first trimester and she says my stomach is bigger than normal or rather than she was. I know Pa will be around again soon and I'm scared I don't want him touching me or even being a part of my pregnancy.

I think about school we should be going on winter break right about now, all the parties that would be taking place, those days are gone, no more hanging out or staying up late I'm a wife and soon to be mother.

I scoot out of bed wincing in pain that's coming from my arm, I look down and notice a bruise there and some marks that look like needle marks what the hell is going on?

I skip going into the bathroom for my normal routine and run across the hall to Amy and Kyle's room I push the door open and see Amy sleeping in the bed no Kyle or KJ. I shake Amy to wake her; she jumps up "Hey what's going on?"

I don't say anything I just flip her arm over, same damn thing "What in the hell did this come from?" I put my arm out next to hers; she looked at it for a while "I don't know I've had these longer than I can remember."

"Where is everyone, It's quite" I said realizing I didn't hear nothing.

I got up off the bed and started walking toward the door when I did hear noises muffled noises. Standing close to the door was Pa and Kyle, and Trey, their backs were to me but Pa was holding KJ looking straight at me, "Good afternoon sleeping beauty," he said smiling.

Trey immediately walked over to me, "What are you doing up?"

"What's that suppose to mean its afternoon, why am I sleeping, and what the hell are you doing?" I yelled.

"Pa is here to do a follow up to make sure things are okay with you and the baby," he said nervously.

I looked from him, to Kyle, to Pa who all looked guilty except for Pa who just smiled. *Creepy*

Even though my first instinct told me something wasn't right I trusted Trey and walked into the room while he helped me into bed. Pa soon followed pushing the ultrasound machine that I hadn't notice when I first seen them.

"Okay this one will be normal, so please lie back and just lift your shirt and pull your shorts under your belly."

I did what he asked and Trey did his normal hold on to my hand but I pulled away, by then Amy and Kyle were standing in the doorway watching this time.

Pa started with the cold gel squeezing it on my belly that made me shiver a little, I closed my eyes again, I know to everyone else it was like I didn't care but I pictured this being a dream or maybe I'm older and happily married with Trey something other than this, then I felt it, "What the hell was that?" my eyes flew open.

Amy walked closer to me, " I seen it on the ultrasound , it kicked" she shrieked "That's not right!" she yelled, "You're not far along for that, your 9 to 10 weeks at the most, you won't feel kicking until about 16 or 17 weeks maybe later," she replied sounding worried.

I was confused I've only been here 3 months, how in the world could I be 4 months pregnant? I know I wasn't pregnant before I got here I had a period, and I wasn't with no one after that, so I'm speechless.

No one said anything they just set there staring at the screen and that's when Pa finally spoke, "We have a problem."

I sat up and looked at the screen and really couldn't make out what I was seeing but to me it looked like more than one baby in there.

"Twins," Pa said excitedly, "a boy and a girl."

Chapter 16

Will you still love me when it hurts?

I jumped off the bed still wet from the gel on my belly, "okay somebody needs to do some explaining now," I screamed.

Pa grabbed his gun out his shirt, walked over and grabbed me by my neck so tight he lifted me off the ground, "you take one step towards me any of you I will shoot her in the head then you one by one," his voice echoed through the room.

I could barely breathe he held me so tight, I started to fight him off grabbing my neck to loosen the hold but he was so strong, he held me by one hand holding the gun in the other, my eyes started to flicker, I gasped more and more for a breath I'm starting to pass out when I hear Trey, "Please Pa, don't do this just put her down and we can talk it over," Trey said calmly.

"Talk it over boy, I did this for you and I'm about up to here with this one's attitude, you get it in check because I hate to miss out on twins," he spit bitterly.

He loosed his grip on my neck and I hit the ground hard I scooted back fast until I hit the wall coughing and gasping for air, I grabbed my neck with one hand and my stomach with the other, wondering if it hurt my babies at all, I said nothing at all I just cried Trey raised his hands in defeat and slowly walked over to me cradling me.

Trey started rubbing my belly while Pa just stood there not moving just staring at us, and then he caught me off guard, "sorry to tell you this but you can keep the boy and I will be taking the girl, if you make it," his voice calm now.

I just cried; there was nothing I could do I had no fight left in me he nearly killed me and them and it was nothing no one could do.

Then Trey slowly lifted me off his lap, "Wait a minute Pa that wasn't the deal," he yelled.

I had to realize what he was saying to him, everything was in a blur.

"Look boy I have no time to play games with you, you knew what could happen so take it or leave it," he hollered.

I could see Kyle trying to shoo Amy out the room but she held on to the doorway entrance, Intrigued.

"You said boy or girl we could keep it if I molded her," he started moving closer to Pa.

"Right," Pa continued yelling, "But you are having both and you know what Ma feels about having them raising the girls, and she is definitely not ready."

By then Kyle grabbed Amy by the hips and moved her out the way, so Trey placed his hand on Pa's shoulder. My mouth dropped. Then he walked him out the room, that's when I realized Trey's not who I thought he was.

Ma…. he put his shoulder on Pa, am I in another universe. I got up off the floor, holding my stomach as I lifted myself to walk over to see what they were talking about, by time I reached the doorway Amy was standing there holding KJ and Kyle and Trey were talking to Pa like they were old high school buddies or better yet father and sons.

"Look Pa Ace has 4 months tops to deliver because she won't go full term with twins, so that gives us plenty of time to get her back on track, please tell Ma to let her keep both, I did this for you guys I wasn't going to take my bride like my brothers did, please I really love her," he said sincerely.

I caught myself smiling in this insanity.

"How will you do that? They're looking right at you," Pa looked at us and smiled.

"The way we have always been doing it," Kyle looked at Amy with guilty eyes.

"The barbiturates," They said in sync'.

"You can't keep giving her them with one baby It's not bad, but with twin she could go into premature labor, and I may be a good medic but I can't sustain premature babies I would have to get rid of them."

The room started spinning my mouth and Amy's mouth were wide open, "There brother's," I whispered to Amy, then I whispered something else, "pretend you are okay with it I have a plan," she nodded then I fell to the ground.

I felt a little disgusted but that's not why I fell to the ground I figure if I distract Trey he will not give me the drug if I act like I'm okay with it, I can be an great actress and one thing I was certain of no matter how crazy he was he wouldn't let anything happen to me or his babies.

Like I thought Trey came running to my side, "Trey, take me to the room I don't feel too good," I said while cradling my stomach.

Trey lifted me up in his arms but looked over to Pa, "This isn't finished."

Trey lightly placed me on the bed, "I'm sorry you had to find out this way, but tomorrow you won't remember a thing, it's for your own good," he replied.

If he was anything like his father, then he is crazy just like him and will respond to crazy, "Trey don't worry, I understand why you did it, I love you and will never leave you, so you don't have to worry about giving me that drug besides I'm scared it will hurt them," I responded softly stroking his cheek.

I knew that's all he wanted me to do is to accept it, and really I don't have a choice I am carrying his babies but that doesn't mean I'm going to let them grow up in this crazy, killer family or even let them get away with it.

"I don't think you will look at me the same way," he said while rubbing the back of his head.

"I told you I wouldn't, besides you did all this for me, who would leave you, you protected me, loved me and the babies, so please trust me when I say I love you," I was very convincing.

Trey started to kiss me on my cheek going down to my neck. I knew I had to make love to him if I didn't he wouldn't believe me even though the thought of touching me let alone in me made me want to vomit but first I had to get what I needed out of him.

"So how many brothers do you have?" he stopped kissing me, then I looked him in his eyes, "I want to know everything about you now that I know the truth," I said starting to kiss him back so he wouldn't get suspicious.

Come to think of it he never talked about his family, but I always into myself never even asked.

He started moving back in the bed peeling off his clothes. I just wanted to barf not because I didn't love him but after all this I do, I just can't believe he's related to Pa. "Well there are 8 of us 5 boys and 3 girls Kyle and I are the youngest Ma and Pa loved children, but these days woman don't want to settle down as they should so Pa was worried about his legacy that's when he came up with this idea 15 long years ago," he trails off.

I wanted to cry; I could imagine how many women were killed, and how many bodies lie buried behind us, so much more than three I'm sure of that.

We continued to kiss while Trey pulled off my shorts; he flipped me over so now he was on top. I knew Trey loved sex, every time we made love he couldn't wait to be in me. Just like now where he jammed in me harder than usual, stroking me harder and harder that I couldn't stop the moaning. Trey was rough he never asked me did it hurt or was he going to fast or hard, he lifted my legs over his head pushing in and out worse than before, I couldn't take it, I told him to slow down but it was like he was on another planet, the wetter I got and the more I moaned the deeper he went. I swear it went on for so long that I knew I would be sore and my mouth was so dry from moaning so loud basically screaming, and then he collapsed on my belly releasing my legs. Tears welled up but I quickly wiped them away so he wouldn't notice.

Trey started kissing my enlarged belly, "now that you know the truth I know Ma will welcome you to the house, like the other girls and my sisters."

So that house is filled with his family, none of them go off on their own they all live together, it's probably because of this eerie secret.

"That would be lovely, I really need to get out of this house for some fresh air, you know," I suggest.

We lay in the bed for a little while when Trey says he has to go talk to Ma and Pa so he gets up and pulls his clothes back on and walks over to the dresser and because he trust me now he opens up the bottom dresser drawer and lifts up a hollow spot where it's a small box he pulls out he opens it and it's filled with syringes that are filled and a single key. *This crazy lunatic had the key this whole time to get out.*

I know the expression on my face looked like a sour lemon because I'm just in total shock, that I fell for this but Amy did too and so did a lot of other people, I hope she's handling it okay because she has been here longer. I smiled when he turned around, "what are those?" I said pointing to the syringes in the box.

He looked at me like I was pointing to a simple clothing item, "Oh these, there just barbiturates 150s," he said simply.

He answered the question like I knew what the hell he was talking about so I gave him the and look.

"Well don't get mad, but these are what we used to put you to sleep for days at a time, I had to start poking you when you wouldn't drink the orange juice anymore, it was laced in it, it also gives you short term memory loss that's why you never knew what day it was."

No wonder why he didn't drink it.

"That's why you weren't sure how far along you are, which is right around 17 weeks which is 4 months and a week and we are hoping that you go full term but that will be a good reason why Ma will not let you stay cooped up in here it's a lot of stress for multiply births," he said while closing the box and placing it on the dresser since it was no need to hide it anymore.

I just really can't believe this is the same gentleman I know and love who deceived me. Why? Because he didn't think I would settle down with him.

"So what day is it then?" I ask hesitantly.

"It's a new year," he says while he walks out the room.

I could about scream a new year, when all along I'm thinking it's December, that must be some strong shit they were dosing me with I hope it has no long term side effects on me and the babies.

I get out the bed and slip my clothes back on and walk out to the hallway just in time to see Trey and Kyle leaving the door, Kyle has KJ in his hands and Amy has tears streaming down her face, then I hear a click and they're gone. I walk back into the room to see them walking in the main house.

Amy slide down on the floor against the wall in the hallway, "I just can't believe this," she whispers.

I'm still standing up so I go to the kitchen to find the pad; it's still in the same spot so they can't be that smart if they didn't realize this is how we have been communicating. I run back to the hallway where Amy sitting in the same spot shaking her head I try to jot down something quick not sure when the guys will come back.

"Amy" I whisper.

She looks up at me with some red puffy eyes, I know that it's hard for her but I don't have time to cry, my only goal is to get the hell out of here.

WE HAVE TO STICK TOGETHER THEY ARE GOING TO LET US OUT OF HERE TO THE MAIN HOUSE, TREY SAYS THAT HOLDS ALL THE WOMEN I WOULD SAY THEY BRAINWASHED , IF WE PLAY ALONG WE WILL HAVE A BETTER ADVANTAGE OF ESCAPING. I shake my hand because I wrote it so fast I got a cramp.

Amy shook her head yes, I knew then she agreed.

She fought back more tears, but wiped the ones that escaped down her cheek, "Kyle told me everything, this is for the best."

Good, if we can trick Trey and Kyle we will be home free. My plan is to escape before my babies come and I have a good Ali, because who know what holds for us in that house, are the women completely nuts or just like Amy and I. Trapped!

Chapter 17

THE Crazy House

Amy and I still stay put on the floor in the hallway it seems like for hours. I start to notice the little ones kicking more, now that I know what it is. Finally the door opens and it's Kyle and Trey, but no KJ they close the door but don't lock it back.

They walk closer to us and we get up off the floor.

Trey comes over and kisses my cheek ,"here's the deal Ma says because we believe you two will not escape they will welcome you to the main house but if there is a slight attitude change at all we will have to return you to the trailers but separately."

I knew we would only have one chance at this as if we get caught there was no turning back so I think this will just be me an Amy's little secret.

"Great when are we leaving," I said sounding overly excited.

"Calm, calm yourself," Trey said rubbing my belly.

"Go grab some of your things Kyle and I will bring the rest over later. The other girls and Ma are getting our rooms ready for us."

I gave Amy a quick glance and followed Trey into the room and she turned and did the same. I was happy to get the hell out of there but even more worried to see what these other people were like let alone be closer to Pa a lot more, and his wife what would she be like? Probably just as crazy.

I finished throwing some clothes in a suitcase Trey had under the bed and eagerly headed for the front door, but not before looking back at the little trailer I spent trapped for months, I stood there for a brief second until Amy and Kyle exited their room, Amy had a look of grief on her face instead of one of relief for finally being free but this is only a ends to a greater means, out of one hell hole into another but at least there won't be no locked doors and the truth is finally out there.

Trey looked at me and smiled, "Are you ready?"

I looked at him questionable, he really doesn't see the wrong in it all, he acts as though we're moving from one house into another willingly like we were happy here and will be happier in the new home.

I just shook my head yes.

I feel like it's in slow motion, he reaches for the door knob, turns it and I could already feel the excitement rising up in my stomach. I'm so close to the door so when it opens the breeze instantly rushes me. Its winter but I could care less; I walk out there in my house shoes finally feeling free, finally feeling the fresh air.

I look back and see Amy so close to Kyle, like being outside scares her, although it has been longer for her than it has for me. I just hope she's not traumatized because I will need her to be strong.

We walk slowly toward the house, I look around for a while, just for a brief second I think to run and don't look back but I know they're watching me and I would be caught before I could even make it to the road but believe me I will be free soon enough. I look back and notice Amy and Kyle walking even slower, Amy has her face buried in Kyle's shirt. The cold wind is blowing so hard my hair is whirling around in my face; I've never felt so free in my life, it makes you realize how you must value your freedom.

I finally made it to the steps of the house, it was huge, and it was bigger than I saw from the window. It was blue and, had a nice huge porch that wrapped around and, a swing hanging from it. The front door was a cherry marble but thick, going down was at least five locks, so I guess not being locked away is out the question.

Walking up the stairs started to give me a slight chill; you would never realize what goes on in this house by the looks of it. First impression is a loving big family lives here, open the door horror, and dig up the yard horror.

I stop once I reach the front door; I feel a little warmth and realize Trey, Kyle and Amy are near.

I closed my eyes for a brief second expecting the worse, but when the door opened up I smelled the scent of home it gave me enough courage to open my eyes to a welcoming face, she stood there with the biggest smile. The woman looked no more than thirty; her hair was brown in a short cut bob, she had a tall slender frame, with dark brown eyes, and pearly white teeth. Her whole demeanor was one of happiness no fear or hate in her eyes.

I felt Trey nudge me from behind, "don't just stand there go in."

I turned around second guessing the whole thing, then I see a still scared Amy ducked away in Kyle's shirt and I knew I couldn't just leave her, if I was going to escape I had to get her and KJ out of here. So I turned and stepped in as the girl moved out the way.

She held her hand out for me, "hello Stacy so glad to have you, I'm Gabriella but everyone calls me Ell."

I step in and hesitantly held out my hand to her, but instead of shaking it she pulls me into a hug that was so warm and comforting I forgot for just a second where I was.

She released me and looked into my eyes, "make yourself comfortable and it will get better."

She then did the same to Amy and when the doors closed there was an uncomforting clicking sound that reminded me just where I was again.

She looked at Kyle and Trey, "I guess my little brothers don't know how to make their wives comfortable, stop standing in the doorway idiots and show them to your rooms."

I could believe my ears, sister it must be one of the sisters he told me about. So now that Amy and I joined in there's 8 families in here not including Pa and his wife, well I could believe it it's big enough, and even though Pa seems old fashion this house is definitely not.

All the floors are a cherry wood that looked like they are waxed everyday; when you walk in the foyer there is a high ceiling with a crystal chandelier with six arm clear crystal glass, with a leaf cut shape that has real candles burning instead of the bulbs that gives it a warm amber glow. Then to your left there's a huge wooden grandfather clock, and right in front a few feet away a stair case that curved up three maybe four floors with a huge landing on each floor.

Trey grabbed my hand and led me up the stairs, we went to the second floor, right off the steps was our room, I thought Amy's and Kyle's would too but they continued up the stairs until they reached the third landing which was the top because it was four levels so it was indeed bigger than you would think from the outside.

I walked in the room that looked like a page right out of better homes and gardens, the bed was neatly made with a orange and green poke-a-dot comforter with curtains to match, the dresser set was wood with a matching armoire and a huge chest at the foot of the bed, and it was a huge green and orange poke-a-dot rug coming from under the bed.

I walked to the bed and set on it, Trey preceded to putting up my clothes in the drawer. I looked around some more and even though the windows didn't have bars on them there was one interesting feature. It was a key lock and I wonder who was the holder of that key, because instantly I knew I could use that to my advantage as far as being pregnant with twins and all, I would get hot on a regular basis.

I guess I seem to be staring out the window so long I hadn't heard Trey call my name, "Ace, earth to Ace."

"Hey….yeah," I quickly turned my head form gazing out the window.

"Pa likes for us to be formal for dinner."

I looked down at what my attire was. I truly didn't feel like coming out the room let alone dressing for an occasion I had no interest attending.

"I don't have any fancy clothes."

Trey walked over to armoire and opened the doors to reveal a row of dresses, different colors and styles.

I turned my noise up, "So now I have to look like a grandma."

Trey started flipping through the dresses, "Ace, I know this isn't your normal attire but you're going to be a mother now so short doesn't cut it anymore."

I studied Trey for a while and wondered if it wasn't the way I dressed what exactly attracted him to me, "So if the way I dressed didn't attract you, what was your interest in me?"

He walked over to the bed and sat down next to me. "I saw something in you, something I knew I would love. I already loved your personality, your aggression and even in this situation the old you is mixed in with the new you."

I knew he wasn't as crazy as he seemed. Even now sitting here on this bed he knew this wasn't right, but why do it then?

Trey got up and walked back over to the armoire he started bringing dress out one by one but each time I made an ugly face, "Okay Ace I'm stumped, what is it you want to wear then?"

"I want to wear this," looking down at what I was wearing, "and I want to stay in this room."

"Please Ace, please don't do this. I promised Ma you wouldn't be such a hard ass about all this. All you have to do is play along. Would you do that for me?"

I wanted to punch him in his head and knock some since into him, that's what I wanted to do.

 I wonder how Amy is doing.

I got in the bed and threw the comforter over my head.

I could hear Trey shuffling around. I peeked out from under the covers to see him going in the chest at the end of the bed, "like it or not you're going."

He placed a nice blue pencil skirt and ruffled blue and white shirt on the bed. It was still old fashioned but way better than that crap he gave me before.

He got up from his knees and closed the chest back, "I'm sorry Ace but believe me or not. I love you and those babies and I'm not letting you go."

He walked out the room leaving me in my thoughts.

Chapter 18

Meet the Collins

I set up in the bed realizing I dozed off, but at least it was from my own free will. I got up out the bed and started staring out the window. Freedom is only inches away. I know I wouldn't be able to jump out the window but at least I would be able to tie a sheet and slide down. I will get out of here and this place and these crazy people will be a thing of the past.

I notice it's a little darker but I know didn't sleep through dinner. Trey wouldn't have allowed it. I realize now he is more like his father than he first took me to believe. His values are strong.

I know it's still him but now I don't feel as bad leaving him and taking my babies.

I get up from the bed just in time to see Trey walking in, "you should be ready. They are setting the tables. Amy and Kyle are already down there."

What am I suppose to happy to know Amy is down there? She's halfway crazy anyway.

Trey walked over to bed and picked up the clothes he had laid out for me, "Look Stacy, I'm trying my hardest to be nice but Ma and Pa went out on a limb for me letting you come here way before any of the other girls."

Now his switch has been officially switched. I could care less about his crazy 'Ma and Pa'. And now where on first name basis.

"How about this Trey I could care less about your crazy ass family, yeah I said it you all are a bunch of nut cases."

He balled up the clothes and threw them right at me, "Well like it or not now you're a part of this family, so get dressed."

I flinched. I never seen him this way he was angry at me. I didn't do anything; he's mad because he tricked me, he lied to me and expected me to accept it because I was pregnant.

I started to take the pajamas I had on off and started changing in the clothes. Tears were streaming down my face by now. I wasn't going to let him break me but I did have to protect myself because if I didn't get out of here before the babies came I had a feeling I wouldn't last long.

Trey watched me until I put all my clothes on then he walked up to me wiping my tears off my face, then he leaned down and kissed my belly, "you two ready to eat? Auntie Ell made a big dinner in our honor."

I rolled my eyes before he leaned back up to me.

"Okay, you ready?" he said reaching out for my hand.

Like I had any choice so I smiled, "Yep."

I grabbed his hand and lead me out the room. I walked down the stairs with him slightly pulling me as we trailed down the stairs; we finally arrived back down to the first floor.

Dragging me we went to the right of the house through some sliding wooden double doors to reveal a modern day dining set, long with a twenty chairs, nine on each side and one to the head of each side.

I was welcomed in by Ell who was still serving dishes on the table full to the rim with food. She was followed by three other girls with matching serving dishes. I looked around the room and no one was scared or out of place but me and Amy who held her head down at the dining table. I could see Kyle trying to lift her head up but if she felt anything like me I wouldn't want to stare in the eyes of the man who kidnapped me or his psycho family.

I did glance at Pa who was sitting at the foot of the table holding KJ and smiling at me, "Please come and sit," he held his hand out to the two empty chairs next to Amy and Kyle.

'Please' It didn't sound like the man I knew just hours ago gripping me up by my neck and holding on until I nearly lost conscious.

Trey continued to pull my arm till I sat down next to Amy and he sat down next to me, so Amy and I were in the middle of the two of them.

Still holding my head down I lifted my eyes up to see the woman at the head of the table looking at me smiling heavily; my conclusion was it was Ma. She was a beautiful woman, which most of the family was.

Ma's face was flawless, no wrinkles, and her brown hair was pulled up in a bun, and her brown eyes seemed to twinkle as she stared at me which gave me the creeps. I quickly looked back down, afraid to look at anyone else.

Trey leaned over and whispered in my ear, "They won't bite."

I just started to cry a little with my head held down, so I could see the tears falling to my stomach that was poked out a bit.

I could hear Pa in the background announcing dinner, "Dinner has been served. I want to introduce the family to our new daughters but because they are shy I will just say their names, no need to stand. Amy is Kyle's wife she has been so for 2 years, and Stacy is the last bride of the baby of the family Trey."

I could feel every one's eyes on me but I didn't look up once. I just continued to let the tears flow.

I then felt a hand on my shoulder that made me jump, "Come on sweetie lets go into the kitchen," Ell said.

I was reluctant to go but she knew I couldn't sit and eat here, I looked over to Trey who just gave me a nod and I got up to leave just as dishes of food were being passed around.

Ell grabbed my hand and walked me through a single door at the right of us to reveal a spacious kitchen, it had all the newest model appliances, as well as wood cabinets with glass doors, marble counter tops and an isle in the middle of the kitchen with five wood bar stools.

She helped me to sit down, she didn't say nothing just started making me a plate of food and sat it down in front of me, "where really excited about twins," she said looking down at my belly.

I wonder what the fascination was with the twins. Their fraternal there's millions of them born every day.

I started to rub my belly, "I'm excited about them too."

She looked at me and smiled, "I'll be right back.

I instantly looked around the kitchen to see if there was a way out, there was a couple of doors my wondering eyes seen but none that looked like a way out only doors to other parts of the house. Then I realized I need a tour of the house that would be the only way I knew how to get out of here.

I was just about to stand and look around when Ell walked into the kitchen with Amy; her eyes were blood shot red.

I knew she had been crying just like I had been. I couldn't help but wonder why Ell was so nice. I could see if she was one of the other girls but instead she's a part of their family, one of them how come she so caring, loving and nice.

Maybe if I play my cards right she will let us go.

Amy walked over and sat down on the stool next to me; I leaned in and hugged her It just felt right. Even though we've only have been knowing each other for such a brief time I still feel like she's my only friend. I can't even stand to be around Trey.

Ell just leaned over the counter top staring at us smiling that's when I knew she was crazy just like them.

She locked at us and she knew we were hesitant to talk to talk in front of her, "I will just go eat with the family, I trust you two alone."

Then she got up and walked out the kitchen leaving me and Amy to plot.

I sat there for a minute thinking of all the crazy things they were capable of. For instance Pa shot Trey; even though he healed quickly they went through all that so he could gain my trust.

I didn't know what route to take, should I just give up, should I just accept this as my life. If I did I wouldn't be me, they would've won, but I can't deny I love Trey he did all this for me although in a sick way he does love me.

I started to feel the twins kick, and realized it's not just me anymore, then I busted out in tears again, "Amy I'm so confused....what do we do? I hate to admit it but I love Trey and I know he loves me."

Amy started rubbing my back shaking her head signaling that she feels my pain, "I know Stacy. I'm so confused myself. I look at KJ and everything is hard all over again."

She leaned in for another hug and we stayed that way until Kyle, Trey and Ell came back in the kitchen.

"I knew this was too much for them," Kyle said walking over to comfort Amy.

Neither me nor Amy parted and they stood there watching us.

Then Ell whispered something, "You two know it was hard for all the girls here when they first came but to go against Ma would be murder."

I had to think about what she said 'Ma' not Pa. I did hear right. Somewhere deep down I knew it was her calling the shots, because what these men wouldn't do for their women.

Kyle grabbed Amy's hand, "come on let's go get KJ and we can go back to our room."

We reluctantly unlocked from our hug and Amy followed Kyle and Trey came and sat down next to me, "You want to go back to our room?"

I looked at Trey in his eyes and shook my head.

Ell grabbed the plate of food I only nibbled on and started wrapping it up, "If you need anything Stacy please don't hesitate to ask."

I nodded my head then Trey walked us out another door which lead us back around to the stairs instead of going through the dining area where everyone was still eating.

I walked up the stairs still silently crying and feeling the twins kick making my stomach get hard.

Once we got to the room I went over and sat on the bed. I hesitated but just asked, "Trey why can't I go home?"

Chapter 19

Getting Informed

I thought it would be smarter if I out right asked him to see how he would react.

He never said a word he just walked out the room.

I scooted back on the bed holding my hands in my head thinking of a way out. I guess it wouldn't be like giving up if I just went along with it. *I must be crazy.*

I quickly got of bed running over to the door to catch up to Trey but I didn't go far I swung the door open to see Trey sitting on the ground outside the door.

"What are you doing?" I kneeled down beside him.

"Nothing just thinking about some things."

I grabbed his arm to lift us both off the ground, "come back in the room we need to talk."

We walked in the room closing the door behind us. Trey walked over to the blue recliner while I sat down on the bed, "There's not much to talk about Ace, you're miserable and there's nothing I can do about it."

I glanced down at my stomach for some sense of courage or explanation and there was none so I just spoke from the heart, "Trey I love you. Why? I'm not sure. You lied to me, you betrayed me but I can't help to think that your love is real."

He got up out the chair and kneeled down in front of me laying his head on my stomach, "I do love you and if you give me a chance I will show you that I'm nothing like them. I held out for as long as I could. I never wanted you like this."

I lifted his head up to see the tears streaming down his face, "Trey let's just run then, me and you. Raise the babies together away from them."

He pulled away and laid his head back on my stomach, "It can't be done."

I just let him lay there for as long as he needed. I felt closer to him than I have in days and call it Stockholm syndrome or whatever I love Trey and I knew he loved me.

A light knock on the door startled us both. Trey got up off my belly and wiped any sign of tears from his face and walked to see who it was.

He slowly opened up the door to Kyle, Amy and KJ. Trey moved to the side letting them in then peeping out the door to see if anyone was around.

Amy sat of the bed next to me holding KJ in her arms.

"So what do we owe the pleasure of this visit," I said lifting KJ out of Amy's arms.

Kyle and Trey traded looks and walked over to us, "We would like to tell you the whole story."

Kyle sat on the bed next to Amy and Trey walked over to the recliner pulling it closer to the bed, "We thought it would make it easier if you knew everything," Kyle said rubbing his forehead.

Trey sat down in the recliner and started fiddling with his hands, "Ma and Pa have been married for 40 years but have been together a lot longer. Their parents were very old fashioned and worse than Ma and Pa. Ma's father was a.... serial killer he killed dozens of women never being caught he died right here in this house."

Amy and I exchanged looks. It was deeper than we realized and the corruption was worse than I knew.

Kyle got up off the bed and started pacing the room, "Ma and Pa were set up by their parents, Ma's father and Pa father were best friends and they wanted their value's passed down from generation to generation. They believed you had to groom a woman before marriage, she had to pass a certain test, and she had to be worth reproducing with. They believed woman in those days were all whores not worth life's existence, at least until you taught them different."

Kyle looked uncomfortable explaining so Trey finished, "They killed mostly women but men too. Ma, Pa and all their brothers and sisters were witnesses of it and those who didn't obey they killed too."

My mouth dropped, "So you mean to tell me they killed their own children?"

Kyle still pacing the floor shook his head yes.

Trey continued, "This is the only reason why we continued the sham. Both Kyle, I, and Janea believe in love, marriage, and respect the same as Ma and Pa but wouldn't kidnap or kill for it. So when we flirted and Pa got his eyes set on you two we had to intercept."

Trey looked at me then my belly, "I swear to you Ace it wasn't going to be this way me and Kyle wanted something different."

"Wait who is Janea?" I asked.

"Janea's my twin or was my twin…," Trey said.

"What you have a twin?" I said shocked.

Trey's voice went down to a whisper, "yes, but she's not here. I haven't seen her in three years, which leads me to believe she's dead."

110

I turned and placed KJ back in Amy's arms and got up to comfort Trey, "but why?"

Trey dropped his head down heavy, "She was not keen on Ma and Pa's ways, and she was, as I and Kyle are the rebellious ones."

Kyle sat back down on the bed, "We went off to college, and we wanted something different we did want a family but in a different way so Trey and I said we would come back with a wife but Janea said she would not marry one of the Barter boys. Their families live as we do so; sometimes I think they're worse."

I didn't know how to take this all in it went further than the 15 years Trey led me to believe. Although I was wrong about him I could definitely see it in his eyes that he was like his father but different in a lot of ways.

Would I regret this? Or would I welcome his untraditional love.

We all sat in silent for a while. I believed it was a lot to take in for us, as well as to speak it out loud for them it had to hit the heart and for Trey to believe his twin was gone probably really hurt and at the hands of his own family.

I rubbed my belly a bit as crouching down comforting Trey was making them kick, "So you all were home schooled till college?"

Trey and Kyle both shook their heads.

Amy finally spoke after being quiet an absorbing all this information, "So how did you and Janea decide to be this way?"

"Well I went to college first and loved it. I was then approved by Ma to even get a job and that's when I met you," Kyle said looking into Amy's eyes. "We talked and flirted and I got to know the inner you, but Pa saw the outer you so…."

We all knew what that meant and I could only imagine what Pa saw me doing.

111

Amy grabbed hold of Kyle's hand with her free hand, "I understand."

"So I was excited by all the business and chaos of the city life and realize it wasn't anything like Ma and Pa lead us to believe, we and everyone else had a choice. So because I was closer to Trey and Janea I couldn't wait to share the things I found out but I wasn't able to speak freely about it to the other siblings and our older brother George Jr. forbid me from coming home until I changed my ways or brought home a wife so I chcose to be with you, instead of them killing you."

So Pa's real name is George and their older brother sounded worse than he did.

Trey cleared his throat, "Janea and I had to keep quiet about what we knew in order to be able to go to college, but once she got there she knew she wasn't coming back and since she was past due in marrying she had made the decision to run away and so she went to school one day and never came home. I choose to believe she ran away but I know better she refused to marry one of the Barter boys so if they didn't get her Pa or George did."

I was happy and relieved to find out he didn't do this to be spiteful, they did this to protect us because they fell in love with us.

Trey lifted me up and sat me down on his lap, "You okay Ace?"

I hugged him so tightly, "I couldn't be better. I now know why you did this. I forgive you; I would be scared of them too."

Amy got up off the bed holding KJ in her arms she walked over to the window peering out of it, "Why don't we just run, why didn't the two of you just run like your sister did?"

Kyle got up off the bed joining Amy by the window, "Believe me I was about to. I had a plan me and Trey and Janea but you came along and I knew once Pa mentioned you it was either go along with it or……"

"So once Kyle brought you home I knew the plan was put on hold but we still planned on it, then Janea and I started college the following year so the

112

plan was going to continue then Ma and Pa were breathing down Janea's neck about William Barter, and Janea despised him and refused to marry him and well once she was gone we kind of gave up."

Kyle stroked Amy's face, "Well we never thought we would love so hard, but we never wanted to hurt you but once Pa has his sights set on you the choice is no longer yours—"

We all jumped. There was a light knock on the door then the door swung open never even giving us a chance to answer. There in the doorway was Ma smiling so innocently when she saw us sitting in the chair together but her smile soon faded when she saw Amy and Kyle peering out the window.

The look of ice that covered her face would make a grown man cry and by the quickness of the boys reaction she wasn't nothing to F*** with.

Chapter 20

The Truth about Stacy

Kyle shifted in front of Amy and KJ and Trey took me off his lap slowly easing up toward Ma, "Hey Ma we were just trying to make the girls comfortable they're use to be around each other."

The expression on her face instantly changed she smile from ear to ear. She slowly walked over to Trey. Bam, she slapped him so hard in the face I reacted without thinking, "Why did you do that? He didn't do anything wrong."

"Oh now she talks. Miss I'm too perfect for this family finally comes out her shell," her voice was as cold as winter on its coldest night.

Her voice instantly stopped me in my tracks, "No Ma'am. I apologize it's just Trey has been good to me and he doesn't mean any disrespect.

She laughed a little, "Well at least my son did something right, you do have some kind of manners."

Trey rubbed his face where his mother slapped him; even though his skin was dark you knew she hit him hard because it left a red hand print.

Trey's voice went down to a whisper, "I...I told you Ma she would be fine, and she will be a great mother."

I could definitely see why they were all scared of her, she was unpredictable, cold, controlling and nuttier than a pecan pie and that combination was a certified narcissist. That made Pa seem much scarier because if he loved a woman like that what else was he capable of doing?

Ma walked past Trey and stopped right in front of me, but he was by my side in an instant, he tried his hardest to shield me but Ma was so close I could smell the left over smell of cheesecake from dinner.

I stood my ground never flinching but she just placed her hand of my stomach still glaring me in my eyes, "I will be the judge of that."

She turned and looked to Kyle with not the same twinkle she gave me her eyes were cold and empty, "You know everyone is to stay in their own rooms if you want to socialize there are plenty of rooms here to do so, so get you and your lovely wife and my grandson out of here now."

Kyle and Amy swiftly walked passed her with Kyle's arm securely wrapped around Amy's back.

"Well have a good night you two. I expect breakfast will be a lot more pleasant."

Ma walked proudly out the room with her head held high and once the door closed I let out the breath I hadn't noticed I had been holding since she approached me face to face.

"How in the world do you guys stand it?"

Trey just stood there in the same spot staring at the door.

I walked to the bed and gazed out the window. I took my tone of voice down a few notches, "Listen Trey I'm not letting her touch our babies so if you don't get us out of here I will."

I knew Trey had a lot on his plate but I wasn't going to let them nut cases anywhere near my babies, but I will play along until the time is right.

Trey finally made a move after standing there for it seemed like forever he never said anything just got into the bed and laid down staring at the ceiling with his arms under his head. I knew he was in thought so I just got in the bed next to him laying my head on his muscular chest, stroking the side of his face that his mother slapped.

115

Trey then moved his arms to wrap them tight around me. In some ways I know I'm grateful for a man as loving as Trey to see what was inside rather what I tried to betray outside. I never wanted to be like this but I guess that was before I knew what it was.

I come from a long history of single mothers. Grandma is a loving woman, overbearing but loving and she lives her life for her children so she didn't have time for a man. I wonder how excited she will be to see the twins.

Mom well I was her only child and she did so much heroine I probably would never k now who my real dad was because she sold her body so much. I tried to block out a lot of the memories of her and her johns but it's hard when sometime I was product of their interest.

I never told Trey about my past about the way mom let the men violate me for money when they thought she was too disgusting to sleep with. I blocked a lot of it out but it only happened a few times before she died although I do remember that night like it was yesterday:

"Stacy I'm going out I'll be back in a few hours."

It usually meant she was going to get a john and bring him back but hopefully she does him there.

"Okay mom but what about dinner?"

"Stacy it's plenty of food in there find you something."

She had the door wide open and she was scratching her arm like she had a mosquito bite that's how you knew the addiction was at its worst so I didn't argue.

"Okay mom, see you later."

She slammed the door behind her and I walked over to the small kitchen in the small apartment that held two bedrooms, a living room that shared the kitchen. I opened the fridge like I thought nothing.

I opened the cabined to find a single pack of ramen noodles.

Better than nothing, I thought. I way far too advance for my age the way I talked and carried myself was more like a teenager than a child but I was more the adult in our household than momma.

I ate my noodles, sat down for a minute to watch some TV. I loved the Simpsons even though it wasn't appropriate for a nine year old grandma always says.

I slowly drifted off excited about spending the summer at grandmas.

I jumped out my sleep to a crashing sound and someone giggling. I already knew it was momma she was drunk out her mind.

"Mom you okay," I said walking over to turn the lamp on.

"Goods... morning.... Sleepy..... Head," her words slurred worse than usual.

I walked over to her to help her steady herself when I saw the man standing in the doorway smiling the lamp didn't do much for the light so it was more like a shadow of a man standing there which creped me out.

I really didn't know if she knew he was there or not, as messed up as she was.

"Hello sir, momma is really wasted I'm just going to lay her down."

He didn't say a word he just shook his head and I walked her in the room. I put her in the bed the best way I could but I have done it so much it didn't really faze me. I stayed in the room with her for longer than I usually did wondering if the man left or not.

I crept to the doorway of mom's room to look out and I didn't see him, so it made me breathe a little easier. I took one more look at mom in the bed she looked uncomfortable yet peaceful.

I went back to the living room to survey it and it was quiet so I turned the lamp off and made sure the door was locked.

I walked back to my bed tired and relieved but it was just another day in this life.

I lay in my bed looking at the ceiling wondering how mom got this way. I really didn't remember much about my life before the chaos but grandma knew mom was getting worse that's why she's been around a lot more and I get to stay with her for the summer.

I finally drifted off.

I woke up to shuffling at first I thought I was dreaming but once I adjusted my eyes I seen the same shadow in the corner of my room.

"I thought you would never settle down," his voice grumbled like thunder.

I sat up it the bed pulling my covers closer to my body, "Sir Momma's room is across the hall."

He started walking closer to me which started to make my body quiver.

He laughed a little, "I know exactly where you tore down mother's room is and tonight I want something new."

I jumped out the bed. Mom never let them do nothing but touch on me she stopped it after that. I know it sounds like I'm making excuses for her but her problem made it so she couldn't make proper decisions.

I moved around the small room a little but he just kept coming closer and closer smiling just like a child molester would.

"Mom could wake up at any moment," I said trying to buy some time.

"Well if she does I have so much heroine at her bedside she wouldn't even notice an earthquake."

I ran for the doorway as quick as I could I was just waiting for him to move closer to me and away from it but I wasn't fast enough he grabbed my arm just as I was going for the knob and swung me in the wall so hard I blacked out.

I woke up on the floor naked and bleeding from my vagina I could barely get up to walk. The sun was shining through the window so I knew I had been out for a while. I shakily walked to the bathroom to shower but that's when I saw her on the floor and I knew she was gone.

"Ace," The sound of Trey voice sent me soaring back to reality.

"Yeah," I said twisting in his arms.

He reached over and wiped the tear that I hadn't notice escape down the side of my face.

"What were you thinking about?"

I sat up in the bed causing Trey to release me out his arms, "I need to tell you some things about me you didn't know."

He looked me in my eyes, "You can tell me anything."

I told him the horrifying truth but instead of him looking at me disgustingly he took me in his arms tighter.

Then he whispered to me, "I promise I will get you out of here if it's the last thing I do."

Trey finally realized I was trapped once in my life and I wasn't going to do it again.

Chapter 21

More Secrets'

The time seemed to drift slowly I was now in my 7 month and we have all been trying our hardest to keep up with the charade. Trey and Kyle went back to school and their regular jobs although they were very skeptical about leaving us in the house alone with the other family members but since that day in the room Ma hasn't came in close courters with me although she still does give me the occasional crazy glance.

I slowly made my way to the bathroom I have been moving in slow motion for the last few weeks I can tell the twins don't have any room but I'm hoping they stay put for a while or at least a few more weeks so they won't be premature. I'm glad to know they are healthy but that is the one time I have to see Pa but he Trey always insist that he is there when he does his examine.

A light knock on the door stopped me in my tracks, "Who is it?"

The door swung open slowly with the smiling Ell peaking around the door, "Hey Stacy just making sure you is getting around okay."

She had been the best person besides Trey, Amy and Kyle of course. I sometime wonder why she doesn't just run herself she seems oddly happy but there's definitely something else there.

"Fine," I said still making my way toward the bathroom.

I left out the bathroom to see her sitting on the bed waiting on me.

"So what's going on?" I said rubbing my enlarged belly.

She got up off the bed looking uncomfortable, "I know since you have been getting bigger it's harder getting up and down the stairs and just wanted to see if you would like me to bring you some breakfast.

I walked over to the armoire to look for something to wear, "No It's okay I can manage."

"Well just yell down the stairs if you need any help."

Once Ell left the room I sat back down on the bed thinking heavily, the time is dwindling down the babies are crowded and with all this unnecessary stress I don't know how much longer they would stay put.

I put on a simple dress that was comfortable even though it was still chilly for May. I made my way down stairs to see the few people that were down there which were mainly the women of the house because all the men were out working. Once again they were old fashioned.

I guess no matter how long George Jr. wife has been here they don't trust them outside alone, they still accompany them out on outings like grocery shopping.

I sat down in my normal spot next to Amy, the dining room consist of Ell, Ma, George Jr. wife, LeAnne who is a bitch it's like she belongs here. Then there's Jordyn that's Brody's wife he's the second born, Harper that's Ethan's wife the 4th born, and Jaslynn the youngest sister besides Trey's twin and she's real quiet just like the rest we hardly get into any conversation and even though Jaslynn doesn't live here she's here quite a bit she lives with the Barter's that usually how it goes the Collin boys live here with their wives and the Barter boys live there with their wives all except Ell of course, I'm not sure why she stays here and not at the Barter house.

I start to talk to Amy when Ma announces that the Barter family will be coming over for a family dinner. I just thought that was horrible from what Trey told me that family is way crazier than his and he doesn't' think there's one family member with their head screwed on straight.

I sat there at the table looking into space wondering how it's going to be tonight. I ate a few more bites of my food and offered to help clean up to Ell but just like usual she turned me down so I headed back to my room.

Since we were now in the main house we now have access to the television so that's what I spent most of my time doing watching movies, catching up on my favorite shows, or reading. I plopped down on the bed and turned on the television to look for a good movie when I stopped on the news. Lately I haven't heard anything in regards to my kidnapping but now after 9 months it finally appeared again and not with a good outcome for them.

It has been nine months since the disappearance of 17 year old Stacy Bellows; she was last seen on September 9th at the Grind House a local coffee shop that is mostly occupied by the local high school kids.

She was last seen with her best friend Natalie Stevens after school on Monday afternoon. Trey Collins the store manager at the time was questioned extensively but then ruled not to be a suspect.

The police are stumped to the whereabouts of Miss Bellows without a single clue the police ruled her a possible runaway but now have been investigating a string of kidnappings in the years and think they are related besides Miss Bellows two teens went missing in the last year 17 year old Alisa Meadows and 18 year old Kailani Mahelona and in previous 2 ½ years 17 year old Amy Landers and 17 year old Melissa Stride. The police haven't found any bodies so they are hopeful that the teens are still alive. If you have any information about these missing girls please contact silent observer.

I sat there with my mouth drew open they showed everyone's picture and sure enough Amy and I were plastered all over the T.V. I knew there have been way more than that in missing teenagers but Trey says because Pa knows just which ones to pick a lot of them are still ruled missing teens or basically runaways.

I wonder if they will still have the dinner tonight because it kind of puts their families in the light extensively.

I just laughed on the inside maybe this is an opening to our plan to unfold.

I lay in the bed slowly drifting off waiting on Trey to come home I missed him so much.

A knock on the door startled me I half expected it to be Ell because she never leaves me alone but when I opened up the door a shocking surprise I had.

She never said a word just looked around and pushed her way in the door closing it softly behind her.

"Don't be alarmed Stacy," Jaslynn said smiling warmly.

I wasn't at all alarmed by her it just shocked me that she was up here and I was intrigued to find out what she had to tell me.

"I'm sorry to bust in here like this but I have to tell you this so you can tell Trey I know how he can get and tonight is going to be crazy."

Once she started talking I got a feel for what type of person she was, she wasn't shy by far she must just kept to herself and looking more at her she reminded me a lot of Ell.

"So where's the fire," I joked.

She cracked a small smile but I could tell this was serious.

"Janea is alive and living with the Barter family," she said while looking me directly in my face.

I sat down on the bed because the twins must have felt my panic because one of them kicked the crap out of me.

"What? Why? How?"

"I can only tell you the clip notes version but needless to say Ma and Pa were on to Janea they knew about her rebellion and married her off to William Barter before she got a chance to run."

I couldn't believe it she was alive and well and Trey and Kyle would be so excited about it.

I too busy being excited about the whole situation I hadn't notice Jaslynn sitting in the chair with her face in her hands.

I pushed up off the bed and walked over to her, "What's wrong Jaslynn this is good news."

"Yeah but from what cost? She sniffled through her hands.

I looked at her but her body was still stiff and she never let her face up from her hands so I kneeled down and slowly moved one of hands off her face. It was already wet with tears and her eyes were red.

"You don't understand Stacy, I knew and so did Ell but we were forbidden to tell any of the other siblings well except George he knew also, you know what they can do to us? Between me and you we are all miserable except George and Ell they're just as crazy as our parents don't get me wrong I love my husband and my daughter but we were forced into this life we never wanted we don't bond , we don't talk we are all mute and act like this is right.

I couldn't believe that Jaslynn felt the same way Trey and Kyle did and they never sat down and talked about it around each other they probably were afraid they would turn on them I really feel sad for this family.

She got up wiped the tears from her face and made her way to the door, "One more thing Stacy, Janea is 7 months pregnant with twins too."

Chapter 22

The Plan

I was in a panic with that news was this a coincidence how is that possible preggers at the same time and with twins. Things are turning bad real quick. Forget the not being in other people's room rule I need to talk to Amy and quick.

I left out the room heading up the stairs, "Where do you think you're going?"

I turned to see LeAnne standing behind me, "Don't worry about it you're not the boss."

I continued to climb the stairs when she grabbed me by my arm and swung me into the stair banister.

"What the hell is wrong with you? Get your hands off me."

"Don't sass me you little bitch. I've been here longer than you and you won't just come in here turning everyone against us."

She got up close to me breathing heavily in my face.

"What are you talking about?"

"Don't act like you're all innocent and happy here I know and soon Ma, Pa, and George will know. You're not obedient enough you will have those babies and they will get rid of you, if not before since Janea is having twins."

She backed out my face smirking. They must have done a number on the pasty colored woman, with cold black eyes. I wondered what George Jr. saw in her she looks like a strung out crack head.

I smiled at that reference it only made her madder and she got back into my face, "I wouldn't laugh if I was you, you think this is a game you don't know how far they will go for family."

Then she pushed me harder into the banister and walked back down the stairs.

"Crazy bitch!"

I walked back up the stairs to the third floor, it looked exactly like the floor I was on, and believe it or not I haven't had the courage to disobey that rule so I stayed to myself these last few months Trey has been back to work and school.

I didn't want to knock on any of the doors afraid I might run into the wrong person so I pressed my ear against door after door until I heard KJ. I knew it was him because no one else had small babies the youngest kid here besides him is Ethan Jr. that's Ethan and Harpers youngest baby, they had the oldest one Amanda while they were in the trailer with Amy so Harper has been here for about three or four years she was one of the older ones because Pa says he tries to get them between the ages of 17 and 19 not to old not too young because then they consider how hard or easy it would be to turn them and train them and how fast they can get pregnant.

I knocked lightly on the door then I heard Amy's soft voice whisper, "Come in."

I walked in the room quickly closing the door behind me.

The room looked just as nice as ours but the whole room had a green theme, windows curtains, bed spread, area rug under the bed all had white and green poke-dots on them and KJs crib sat in the corner of the room with green Winnie the pooh bed sheets, comforter and mobile.

"What are you doing in here?" Amy whispered to me.

"I need to talk to you it is very important," I said with my back leaned against the door.

126

"You know if they catch us there will be some bad repercussions so hurry," Amy said while bouncing KJ up and down on her hip to quite him down.

I stood by the door afraid someone might come in just to get a quick getaway.

"Well long story short Janea is alive and living with the Barter's she is married to William Barter and also expecting twins and most of the family knows except a few family members not quite sure who."

Amy sat KJ down in the crib and walked over to me, "Wait, wait, wait a minute who told you this and why now?"

"Jaslynn told me because you know she lives at the Barter house; she has been taking care of her and afraid that if she told they would do something to her and her son."

"So why now?"

"The family dinner."

Amy stood there for a minute absorbing it all in as I did.

"I think tonight is the night we get away because once I tell Trey things are going to heat up and the fact his family never told him, so Amy keep KJ close."

I opened the door and peeked out, "I gotta go but if you want to tell Trey go right ahead. I think I will let Trey see for himself because if I tell him now it will ruin the getaway. I know if anything happens he will find me, but I got to get out of here and he has been taking his sweet time doing it."

"Oh one more thing, watch out for LeAnne she's out for blood."

I walked out the room and crept down the stairs but instead of going back to my room I went to the kitchen for a snack.

The downstairs was empty which was odd it was always one of the girls in the kitchen if not Ma. I got the pops out and the milk, I poured the milk in a cup of ice because I hate to eat cereal in warm milk, my milk has to be freezing. I let the milk stir in the ice for a minute then poured it over my cereal. I squeezed my way on the stool the best way I could and started munching down my cereal. Still the kitchen remained quiet. I was curious to where everyone was so I finished up my cereal and wondered the house something we weren't allowed to do but hey I've been breaking all kinds of rules today.

I tip toed my way through the house, the living area, the library, still nobody then I started to hear whispers further down the hall coming from Ma and Pa's study where nobody was allowed.

"Pa's on his way home with George. They will want to put the girls back in the trailer because of the news.
Who will go back? Amy, Stacy, and Harper, I think Jordyn will be fine."

"You really think you have to put Harper in there, they never mentioned her on the news she's been here a little longer?"

"Yes, I know Ethan will be made but I know these girls I've spent time with them."

"Well okay it's settled we will put them in there after dinner tonight, it's no since in canceling the dinner because the Barter's are already set on coming but we best not tell the boys."

I recognized the voices it was Ma, Ell, and LeAnne. I knew she wasn't to be trusted. Like hell they're putting me back in there to deliver my babies.

I heard shuffling sounds and ran as fast as I could around the nearest corner just in time to see LeAnne peak her head out the door then Ma walked out, "What's wrong?"

"I thought I heard something, "She said still looking around.

"No one is allowed down these halls except for you and the rest of the family the girls aren't allowed down here and they know it so stop jumping to conclusions."

But Ma was wrong and LeAnne stood there for a minute then walked back in the office with her. I ducked out my hiding spot back down the hall and up the stairs. I didn't breathe until I reached my room and closed the door behind me. I jumped in the bed and pulled my covers over me, I was afraid to go back there I really don't think I would survive I just need a plan and quick—

I felt the worst sharp cramping pain ever. Oh my God..... I can't be going into labor just yet. I think I just over worked them. I will just lay here until the pain passes and sure enough it did enough for me to drift off finally.

The sound of rustling woke me up, I wasn't quite sure how long I had been out but when I adjusted my eyes it was Trey throwing some of my clothes in a bag, "what are you doing?

"I have to get you out of here now. I know they are planning on putting you back in the trailer and I won't be able to be with you this time so now is our time to go. Its last minute but I got a plan."

"How did you know they were planning on doing that?"

Trey continued to stuff as much things as he possible could in the bag, "The news Ace, the news."

He must have been watching the news work this noon hour and came right home but still.

"Trey, stop now and explain."

Trey looked up from the duffle bag to look me in my eyes; he dropped the bag to the floor and walked over to me probably sensing my panic.

"I'm sorry Ace but I have to get you out of here, you see this happened once before to George Jr., Brody and Ell. The girls got put back in the trailer

129

because of the news footage this was about around the time Pa and Mr. Barter were going crazy kidnapping and killing before they got their routine down and this was the one time Ell had to stay with the Barters she was pregnant the stress of it all made her lose the baby and she wasn't never able to get pregnant again."

Now everything makes since I never knew, nor wanted to ask but I did know it was something.

"Listen grab your stuff from out the bathroom and we will be on our—"

There was a knock on the door mid-sentence.

"That must be Kyle and Amy. I told Kyle to meet me home but he wasn't here when I got here."

Trey walked to the door to open it while I got our toothbrush and deodorant out the bathrooms but it wasn't Kyle or Amy at the door it was George Jr. so Trey instantly waved me back in the bathroom before he saw me.

"Why are you home so early? He said pushing his way in the room.

"I could ask you the same thing, "Trey said confidently.

"Well quick family meeting about dinner with the Barters."

"That's funny no one mentioned it to me."

"You know Ma doesn't like to pull you out of work or school if it's not important."

There was silence for a minute then George Jr. spoke again.

"Where's that wife of yours?"

"She's in the bathroom; you know how those pregnant bladders are."

"Oh okay. Well dinner will be late tonight instead of 6 it will be 7:30 I just wanted to let her know because that one loves to eat."

"Thanks I will pass it along."

I heard the door close and came out the bathroom, "What was that all about."

"He was checking up on us. Damn I know when Kyle comes in he will know something is up."

Trey paced the floor, "Think Trey, think."

"It's okay we will be fine." I said walking over rubbing his back.

"That's the thing we're not, if they get desperate enough they will get rid of everyone they think is a threat. The news never named everyone like they did today and for the fact they are coming over later than sooner only tells me that."

"What Trey?"

"They plan on getting rid of all of us except for probably the first born and their wives."

"Wait when you say us, you mean the children too?"

Trey only dropped his head low. I pulled him in a hug and he held on to me tight.

"Trey if we tell the others they will run then we will be able to overpower them.

Trey looked up like a flash of lightning popped in his head, "I have a plan."

I hope it's a good one because I hate to tell him he found his sister to only lose her in the same night.

Chapter 23

An Uncomfortable Feeling

"I will be right back I promise."

"But Trey I'm scared," I said holding on to him tight."

He grabbed hold of both my arms tight and looked me in the eyes, "They will have to kill me before they hurt you and those babies, do you understand me?"

I shook my head yes with tears streaming down my face. Trey was my love and I know he would die twice before he put harm upon me and these babies and I love him even more for that. Trey took me into a warm hug and I didn't want to let him go but then he released me and closed the door behind him and I felt a wave of nausea come over me, I had to sit down on the bed and that's when I was hit again by a contraction. It was a little more painful than the one I had earlier. I think all this stress is getting to the babies. I need to calm down so I got back into the bed to rest still staring at the door watching for Trey.

My eyes began to get heavy but I wasn't going to fall asleep until Trey was back and I knew he was safe. I started to hear a lot of talking which made me a little eager, I'm not quite sure how much time had passed but I was happy for him to be back. I continued to hear the voices then they got louder and I was able to make out the voices and neither of the voices was Trey's but they were familiar.

"Listen Ethan she will not have to be in there long but Ma and I feel it is better for our family's safety."

"Why not Jordyn too, Harper is older than her?"

"If you would like to argue with Ma then go right ahead."

I can't believe how sneaky LeAnne is being she is the one who suggested Harper not Ma. Wow I wonder who really is pulling all the strings.

I listened a little more before they drifted down the hall but from what I heard Ethan wasn't happy and this was great for me because the more unhappy the family members were the easier it will be for us all to rebel.

I got up off the bed to be noisy but as soon as I made it to the door it swung open quickly.

"Hello there, just a quick check- up," Pa said dropping his medical bag to the ground.

His creepy voice nearly made me throw up then the smile he had gave me the creeps.

"Where's Trey he's always with me," My voice shivered just a little bit.

"Well I haven't seen him and that doesn't mean neglect the baby right."

I wasn't sure if they were trying to be funny if they called him or just let me call him he would be here in a flash.

"Well I would like it if Trey was here so don't come near me."

Coming from behind Pa was George Jr. this can't be good, "Don't be difficult Stacy."

I rolled my eyes at both of them making sure they both saw, "I'm not trying to be difficult but I'm not letting you touch me without Trey."

I walked back over to the bed gazing out the window wondering where in the hell Trey went he never said he was leaving the house. Then my stomach began to drop…. I hope they didn't do anything to him.

I started to walk towards the door when George grabbed my arm, "Where are you going?"

"I'm not sure if you two are deaf or just stupid but I said you won't be touching me without Trey being here so get your grubby hands off me."

I never saw it coming; I just fell to the floor holding my face.

"Boy why'd you do that she's pregnant where tryna keep the babies in not cause her to go in labor early."

"Well the little bitch needs to learn some manners Pa, you taught me that."

George lifted me up off the ground and threw me on the bed he started pulling my dress up and ripping my panties off I screamed, "Stop what are you doing?"

"Calm down we're not doing anything to you we need to check and see if you dilated yet."

I started pushing his hands off of me, "No don't touch me."

Pa came around to the other side of the bed to grab my other arm I'm still pushing and yelling at them when Ell bust in the room, "What the hell is going on."

I never heard her talk like that so it made me stop in my tracks.

"We're trying to check her but she won't be still, George said still holding me down."

"Have you not learned yet that all this stress is not good for the babies' just move out the way?"

Ell walked over to me and sat on the bed I embraced her in a hug and she started to calm me down while Pa and George stood watch. She pulled me out the hug to see the side of my face that had already swollen up, "What happened here."

I just looked over at George, "George is what happened here."

"Listen Stacy we need to check on the babies so I will stay here and watch and George will go get you some ice," she said giving him the evil eye.

What is going on? I'm so confused who is who in this crazy family? I need Trey I can't take this any longer.

George huffed a little then walked out the room leaving me with Ell and Pa. Ell eased me on the bed and rubbed my shoulder to make me comfortable while Pa walked over to his bag and pulled out some gloves.

I lay back on the pillow and closed my eyes. I was truly scared I didn't know what to do but my body automatically stiff up when he put his fingers in my vaginal and started feeling around. Ell grabbed my hand and I squeezed it with all my might while tears fell down the side of my swollen face.

"It will be okay just relax," She whispered in my ear.

I still held my eyes closed shifting with the pain of him pushing in there harder and harder to the point it got even more uncomfortable I mean I never had any one feel for dilation but it shouldn't take that long.

"Well Pa," Ell said impatiently.

"She seems to be at 1 ½ which is normal for multiple births she will have some pressure because of the multiple straining, and they seem to be both head down. So far I don't see any complications." Pa removed his hand out of my vagina taking the glove off and heading toward the bathroom.

"Great!" Ell said a little too eager.

Pa came out the bathroom drying off his hands with one of the bathroom towels, "She should rest until dinner."

"Okay we're going to let you get some rest;" Ell fluffed my pillows and pulled the blanket that was at the foot of the bed over me."

Pa walked over to his bag picked it up and walked out the room just in time for George to walk in with the ice pack he handed it off to Ell never saying one word to me.

Ell handed me the ice, "Keep this on your face for as long as you can it won't look so swollen about time dinner rolls around.

I grabbed the ice and applied it to my face; Ell started to walk out the room, "hey Ell, as soon as Trey comes in can you please tell him I need him."

Ell shook her head yeah and walked out the room closing the door behind her leaving me alone in the silence.

Times like these I miss my grandma and my friends, I never realized how I took people for granted, how I would suffer from my actions.

I started to cry wanting to be rid of this life. I never felt suicidal but I never depended on just one person either and Trey is my lifeline right now without him I wouldn't even have had a fighting chance.

I looked down at my belly and start to feel guilty. There I go again just thinking about myself I have to live for them and fight for them too but they sure know how to break a girl's will real good.

I start having more and more contractions and they start to get consistent but still tolerable but for how long. I almost get out the bed to go find Amy or someone I trust when my heart dropped when Trey came through the door.

"Oh my God Trey, Where have you been? I've been here crying and thinking bad things and not to mention…." I had to think about that I didn't want Trey to know I have been having contractions he would probably change his plans so I just kept quiet.

"What the hell happened to your face?"

Oh wow I almost forgot about George slapping me. I know how his temper can get so I won't tell him.

"This?" I said pointing to my face, "this is nothing. I wasn't watching were I was going.

Trey walked over to me and lifted my face up and side to side, "Now are you really going to lie to me? Now the question is who did this to you?"

I looked down to the floor not able to look Trey in his eyes, and then a tear escaped from my already red puffy eyes.

Trey lifted my face back up so my eyes met his again, "Ace who did this to you."

"George," Then I couldn't hold them back no longer instead of the silent sobbing I had been doing I was in full cry baby mode but Trey just pulled me in and let in all come out.

I told him what had happened and it only fuel to his already angry fire so I will hold in the pain of the contractions until we leave because by the look on his face when he did come in the room good news is ahead.

Chapter 24

I smell freedom

Trey walked over to the armoire where he hid our bags and pulled them out, "Trey when push comes to shove grabbing bags will be the last of our worries."

He stood there in thought for a minute, "Your right skip the bags I hold on to you and you to me that's all we will need, but please promise me one thing if you look back and I'm not there you promise me you will keep going."

I was not sure what he was trying to ask me, leave him I would never do that.

I walked to the window gazing out at the cornfield that's across the road, "sure Trey I'm just going to leave you."

Trey stuffed the bags back into the armoire and walked over to me, he placed his hand on my back rubbing it gently, "You can't think about us anymore," he moved his hand from my back to my stomach, "you have to think about them do you understand me."

I knew Trey was right and I knew I had to listen to him but I just couldn't even imagine raising these babies without him.

"Trey how were we going to get out of here anyways," Trey looked out at the cornfield then back at the door then he made his voice barely a whisper, "Kyle and I got this truck from a friend of his in one of his college classes we had been sneaking money to save for it for months now because Ma and Pa collect most of our wages and then the rest goes in a family pot for household finances, so he parked it out beyond the cornfield and once we get through the cornfield it's easy sailing from there, we will get you guys as far as possible away from here."

"But how will we even get out the house?"

"You just leave that up to me I have everything all worked out."

I was excited and scared all at the same time many, many things could go wrong but if we make it through this we can make it out with ours and our babies lives intact.

A knock on the door scared the hell out of both of us, as Trey was holding me and we both were gazing out the window looking to the future.

Joslynn walked through the door before either of us got a chance to answer it. She rushed in panting like she was out of breath, "Did you tell him?"

It nearly slipped my mind about the whole Janea thing, but would telling him ruin it all? Will Trey or Kyle want to leave after learning the truth?

Trey released me from his hold and walked over to his sister who was still panting heavily, "Told me what? Is everything okay?"

Joslynn looked from me to Trey. I knew she saw the look of a deer getting caught in a head light look on my face.

She opened back up the room door, "Dinner is served, and they're all here," she looked directly at me.

"That's it? That's what I needed to know?"

Joslynn walked out the room to the stairs realizing I didn't tell him but I wonder if she knows why.

I usually go barefooted but since I wasn't coming back here I slipped on some pajama pants and the only shoes I do own which are some house shoes and walked back towards Trey.

I grabbed his hand and led him out the room, "you will see."

I know he was reluctant on what was before his eyes but I couldn't tell him he had to see for himself.

We trailed down the steps to hear a mass of talking: it was so loud I thought I would lose him so I grabbed his hand tighter as we walked down the steps with Joslynn leading the way.

Once we got down the stairs right in front of the foyer, I knew Trey saw the same thing I did because you cannot mistake the resemblance. I know it sounds weird but Janea reminded me of myself, her hair was brown like mine but flat which is the same way mine had been looking for the last 9 months because of the lack of beauty supplies, although LeAnne pasty face is always made up. I wonder who gives her the authority to look like that.

Trey's mouth dropped open and I could tell he was surprised because he squeezed my hand so tight that I nearly screamed but with all the commotion that was going on it wasn't like anyone would hear me anyways, he started pulling me down the stairs with him passing Joslynn as she lead us until he was face to face with his sister and her husband with her belly sticking out just as far as mine.

Looking at her face I could see right through her and she was me. Her eyes showed a cover-up but I could tell but I wasn't quite sure if William Barter was crazy like them and if she really even loved him but she sure did have her hand placed on her belly in a protective way.

The Barter's were big just like Trey, Pa and his brothers these were big men which made you come to the conclusion they must have knew what they were doing when they decided to do this because for one, as a big person you can overpower someone quicker that you would as a smaller person.

Trey yanked me through the crowd of crazy family members to get to Janea but Ma started moving folks into the dining area which was made up differently today it had more tables to accommodate all the family members that came today, they had two more tables that were round that could sit 4 to 6 people.

Most of the older kids set at those tables but I instantly seen how Ma set them at the table with George Jr. and LeAnne's older sons.

Trey never removed his eyes off of Janea while he pulled the chair out for me. I scanned the room and no Pa or George Jr. they must call their selves getting the trailers ready but they sure will have egg all over their faces when they see what happens. I still wasn't sure how we planned on leaving he never told me that bit of information because the doors are always locked you have to have a key to get in and out and only a select few hold that key and from what Trey has told me Ma, Pa, LeAnne, and George Jr. hold the key not even Ell has a copy.

The sound of Ma clearing her throat brought everyone to attention, "I would like to give thanks to the good Lord for bringing our families together tonight and for keeping all our children safe."

She had the nerve to thank god for bringing us together. It always surprises me how crazy this family is. Joslynn, LeAnne and Harper start to bring in dishes of food setting them on the table. They had so much food I nearly jumped out my chair, just the fat girl in me talking.

Pa and George still hadn't arrived yet and it made me nervous I kept giving Amy glances but neither she nor Trey was alert. Trey was starring oddly over at his sister and Amy kept an eye on Ma who was having a deep conversation with Ma Barter.

I wanted to get out of here and Kyle and Trey never fully explained the plan. I stopped abruptly when I heard a silent vibration. It was a phone but where was it coming from? Ma got up from the table with Ma and Pa Barter, this gave me a chance to nudge Trey out of his trance and whisper in his ear, "What's going on? We need to get going post haste."

Trey looked around like he didn't know where he was, "It's covered don't worry about it but it's a slight change in plan, Janea's coming. I'm not leaving my sister here to turn out like them."

I was very confused to when he came up with that plan, they never talked, and how did he even know she wanted to go with us. Did they have that secret twin telepathy everyone always thinks twins have? No that's crazy, but they were staring at each other for a while.

I was just about to ask him how in the world he knew she wanted to come when Ma came in the dining area with her face drew down and sweat on her brows, and that was a look of nervousness. Yes something happened we are well on our way out of here.

Ma cleared her throat, "Ladies please grab your babies and hold tight to your children we have a small problem and we need to step outside in the yard."

I nearly pissed my pants when she said that, we actual have to step outside it's that bad. Trey grabbed my hand and gave it a little squeeze that signaled me things we going as planned.

Chapter 25

All Hell Breaks Loose

Once Ma had all of us in a line ready to go outside she pulled out her key from out her blouse that was attached to chain around her neck and unlocked both locks on the door.

I walked out the house holding Trey tight and immediately the smell of something grilling evaded my nose I haven't smelled it in so long it started bringing back memories of home and summer and how grandma said the best part of summer was eating a hotdog off the grill. The sky was at that point when the sun is down but you could still see the clouds in the sky although they were dark blue with a hint of black.

I felt like we were being pushed out the house but who's complaining. Once we got down the stairs, the older Barter and Collin boys minus George Jr. started putting us in a circle so close and tight we were just about touching each other and I knew Ma's intentions were to keep Trey away from his sister but in all the chaos that didn't work they were so close her hand touched his and at that moment I knew she was coming with us if that was the last thing Trey was gonna do.

Once we were in the circle talking and in a panic Ma Barter spoke, "We have a trader in our mist and those who betray our family will surely suffer the consequences." Her voice reminded me of an evil witch on Halloween, shrill and scary.

Trey's hand locked into my fingers tighter than before that I nearly lost all circulation. Babies were crying and kids were complaining about the chill of the late May evening.

Then I heard shuffling coming from the side of the house like something being dragged. It was Pa and he was dragging something. Oh my God he was dragging a person. I turned my face down to the ground afraid of what was going to happen.

I heard a shot which made me look up. It was George Jr. holding a shot gun and he fired it up into the air then Pa spoke.

"Anyone here know this gentleman? I saw him running away from this house but he wouldn't tell me what he was doing here."

Everyone froze but I had the inkling that Trey or Kyle knew exactly who he was. The black in the sky started getting darker and darker first I thought maybe it was getting dark but then the smell of smoke started to get stronger then I realized it was a fire not bar-be-cue. Did they know?

Pa started dragging the guy closer to the circle everyone was in and I could see he was still alive because he was moving and trying to get away from Pa, "Stay still boy or I will shoot you dead." That didn't stop him from squirming until George Jr. pointed the gun straight to his head. "Now tell us what you are doing here and who sent you," Pa asked again.

The guy was stubborn but he spoke, "You old country hicks the police is on their way and as we speak and your house is going up in flames."

Pa was still holding him tight but he waved George Jr., Brody, and Anthony Barter around the house but before he left George Jr. handed Pa his shot gun.

Anthony came running to the front seconds later. "It's a full fledge fire blazing back there. Where do you keep the fire extinguishers?"

Ma ran back into the house with Anthony and came flying back out with two fire extinguishers they ran back to the back of the house not saying one word.

Pa then dropped the guy and turned the gun on him, "Now tell me what I want to know or this will be the last time you breathe."

By then everyone was on edge the guy got up off the ground holding on to his side because it looked like he got a whoop down from Pa and George Jr., "You know how you like to stalk and watch your victims, oh and terrorize your family. I'm the one doing that to you the police should be here any second but the thing of it all, it was all worth it. No one will ever go through this again."

Then he shot off running toward the cornfield then Trey took my hand and put it in Janea's hand and yelled now, she looked at me for it seemed like eternity but only seconds passed and me and her darted our way toward the cornfield only stopping when a shot ran out, we turned briefly to see the guy falling down to the ground with his guts splattered out in front of him while Pa stood holding the shot gun that smoked from it like a chimney fire.

Trey yelled again and we held each other hands tight and continued until we reached across the street then I stopped right in front of the tall cornfield to do something Trey told me not to do but I had to see if he was coming but instead it was Amy running towards us holding KJ tight in her arms, then sirens started coming from all over I wasn't sure if we should stay or go and then we were caught off guard by LeAnne's pasty ass, she grabbed Amy by her red flowing hair and yanked her so hard she almost dropped KJ. Janea instantly let go of my hand and right hooked LeAnne so hard she fell to the ground which freed Amy and I signaled for her to keep running, so she darted off through the cornfield leaving Janea and I standing there with a busted nose LeAnne, "I couldn't wait for that, you evil Barter."

I looked down at LeAnne who still wore that sneaky smile through her busted face, "Barter! She's a Barter? I thought they just had boys." I was shocked! So they kept us in the dark on purpose? No wonder she was a bitch although she never hid that.

"Yeah she's the eldest Barter and just as crazy as the rest of them."

LeAnne grabbed her nose and started wiping the leaking blood, "You think you will get away you got another thing coming."

Janea just looked at her with the coldest eyes and spit right in her face and grabbed my hand and we ran as fast as our pregnant bellies and legs led us.

We made it halfway through the cornfield when I stopped, I was panting heavily and so was she and the contractions I had been having started getting stronger. Janea was as sweet and loving as Trey describe and just like him, she pulled me in a hug and I started to sob a little thinking to myself I may never see Trey again. Janea grabbed my other hand and we stood there for a brief moment staring at each other.

Janea wiped the single tear that escape out her eye and rolled down her face, "he would want us to go on for them."

Yeah they were definitely related.

I started hearing gun shots and sirens getting louder and louder and even though I knew reinforcements were near we still continued running.

I knew relief was near when I saw a shadow of a SUV right at the edge but relief was short lived, "I knew you were acting weird all day and to think my own sister would do my wife like that." The cold voice of George Jr. sent chills down my neck. I really would have thought the police or Trey and Kyle would have held him off.

"Now the two of you stop in your tracks or I will put a whole in each of those bellies."

I wanted to bend over in pain because the contractions were right on top of another but Janea and I just raised our hands in the air and turned around slowly. It was just about dark so we could barely see the shadow of him but I sure saw that shot gun in our face, "now come closer, we have to find a way out of here."

George started looking around. I was hoping he wouldn't notice the truck....

Someone was near the rustling in the cornfield got louder and quicker so George Jr. turned quickly taking the gun off of us. I was hoping it was reinforcements and it was. Kyle leaped in the air and started trying to fight the gun out of George Jr. hands but he was just as strong. I grabbed Janea's hand and headed for the truck. Pow!

The sound of the shot gun echoed through the field and all of a sudden I felt heaviness in my hand. I looked down to see Janea holding her stomach, "No…. Get up Janea." I lifted her up the best I could and pulled her back to the truck. I could barely see. It was dark and tears started welling up in my eyes.

I opened the door to see Amy ducked in the backseat with KJ rocking back and forth, "Amy where are the keys?"

She peered up and her mouth dropped. It was so much blood from the gunshot wound I didn't know exactly where it was coming from.

Amy jumped over the seat and put KJ in the passenger seat and searched for the keys, we knew they were in there because they said they would be hid in here depending on which one of us made it.

Amy pulled down the visor and they fell out, "You know how to drive?" I yelled out to her while pressing my hand against Janea's bleeding wound.

"Yeah," she said starting to cry.

Amy roared the ignition when we heard a bang on the car. I thought it was George Jr. but it was Kyle, he walked to the passenger side and grabbed KJ and jumped in, "Now Amy, we have to go now."

Amy put her feet to the gas and shrieked out of there, "Turn right." Kyle said pointing in that direction.

"We're not far from the local hospital."

I looked down at Janea for the first time and she seemed to be peaceful she still was breathing but she wasn't conscious.

"How is she?" Kyle said leaning over the seat.

I just looked up at him and shook my head. I didn't know.

When we first left I didn't know where we were but now looking up I knew exactly where we were and thank goodness the hospital wasn't far.

"Make a left." Kyle told Amy.

Just as we were pulling into the ER the police were behind us.

Amy put the car in park and jumped out; she opened the passenger side door and slowly lifted Janea's head. Just as we were getting out both the cops and hospital attendees started coming.

"Please she was shot and she is 7 months pregnant," I shouted while also bending over in agony myself.

They escorted us in putting Janea's still body on the gurney and shuffling off yelling hospital code in the distance.

I couldn't breathe my head felt heavy. I started hearing noises from everywhere police asking me questions, Kyle yelling while police were grilling him. Everything was now in the distance like I was in a fog, "Ma'am what is your name? What is the young lady's name with the gunshot wound?"

Then one of the nurse's put me in a chair and bent down at my eye level, "Ma'am take deep breathes and tell me what happened."

I began to explain what I could and the clip notes version, she immediately dispatched the nurse to take me to a room to set me up on a monitor.

I felt a warm touch to my shoulder and looked up to see Amy holding KJ, "It will be okay honey, I am right here.

I tried to speak loudly but my voice was barely a whisper, "Where's Kyle?"

She looked over her shoulder to the police who were questioning Kyle, "he's answering some questions but I tried to clear it up the best I could.

148

Once the nurse hooked me up to all the baby monitors I asked Amy to go see how things were with Janea and Kyle, she shook her head and walked out the room.

I laid there for a brief moment when one of the nurses came in the room, "how are you feeling sweetie?"

I scooted up in the bed, "the contractions are strong; am I in labor?"

The nurse looked down at the monitor, "we seem to think so from all the stress your body has been in so the doctor is going to come in and check you and we are going to give you a steroid shot because at 7 months the baby's lungs might not be fully developed."

"Babies," I said rubbing my belly.

"Twins ma'am?"

"Yes, and its Stacy, Stacy Be…Collins."

"Mrs. Collins, do you know about how many weeks you are?"

That was a good question I briefly lost track. I knew I was 7 maybe close to 8 months.

I shook my head to her.

She jotted down a few notes and walked toward the door.

"Nurse, can you tell me the status on the girl who came in with me?"

She turned back around walked back towards me, "As far as I know she is still in surgery but they did get one baby out, a boy."

As soon as she opened the door up Amy was walking back in still holding KJ.

Amy sat down in the chair next to the bed, "they wouldn't tell me much but she still in surgery which is a plus."

I rolled over in the bed facing her, "the nurse just told me they got one baby out safely a boy but she didn't give me any more information. God I hope she is okay."

KJ started to fuss a little while Amy was rocking him, "I think he might be hungry. Do you mind?"

I shook my head and turned back flat in the bed.

Just as Amy was getting KJ comfortable to breast feed two men came into the room, one was tall with a bushy mustache and copper skin and the other was just a shy shorter than him with a clean shaven face and a bald head and even though they weren't dressed as cops I knew they were, "I'm detective Karl", said the tall officer with the bushy mustache showing his badge.

"And I'm Detective Louis," said the officer that was a little shorter than him with the bald head.

Detective Louis took a pad from out his coat pocket, "Mrs. Collins we need a few words with you."

I placed my hand over my stomach and looked over at Amy, "Which one of us do you need?"

The detectives looked at each other, "You're both named Collins? Are you two sisters?"

Even though Amy and I are obviously different races it's still a valid question.

"No sir", Amy said lifting KJ over her shoulder, "we are married to brothers."

The two detectives walked closer to us, "We need to know what happened and please don't leave anything out."

Detective Louis clicked his pen he had, "but first I need your maiden names."

Chapter 26

The Truth shall set you free

This was our out, we finally are home free, but why do I have this horrible feeling? The contractions were getting strong and I wanted them out of here. The nurse was no were to be found with any type of medicine.

Amy got up from the chair, "Detectives we can talk out here, as you can see Stacy is in labor and I can tell you everything you need to know. With starters my name is Amy Landers and this is Stacy Bellows and we're kidnap victims."

Both the detectives walked toward the door opening it up and gesturing for Amy to walk through but before she left she walked over and kissed my forehead, "I will be right back and I will send a nurse in here I can tell the contractions are getting stronger."

The three of them walked out the room leaving me in the silence of the hospital room with only the small echo of the twin's heart beat on the monitor to comfort me.

The only thing that went through my head was Trey. I shouldn't have never left him, I felt empty I knew they would have killed him for betraying his family but I am his family the twins and I. Why in the world have they not mentioned what happened at that house and the other children are they even okay?

The nurse walked in the room with the doctor followed by he was a tall handsome doctor he looked to be no more than 35 but I knew being a Doctor and all he had to be way older than that. His tanned complexion was flawless and he appeared to have no wrinkles, "Mrs. Collins we need to check and see how far you are dilated."

I shook my head and they proceeded to prep me to take a look.

I squeezed my eyes shut tight as I always did when Pa did the same thing but this time I felt empty, Trey was always by my side making sure I was okay, holding my hand. Tears started welling up in my eyes. That's when I felt the warm touch of the nurse's hand on my shoulder.

"Okay all done Mrs. Collins," He removed his gloves and threw them in the nearby trash can.

The silence in the room was eerie he kept looking down at the monitor then my chart, then started feeling my stomach not once looking at me directly which started to make me nervous.

"So doctor what's the verdict?"

The doctor walked up to me and held his hand out which I hadn't notice how hairy they were, "I'm sorry I didn't introduce myself I'm Dr. Walburn and this is nurse Leena as you already met. It's been a busy night. Well you're dilated to 5 which means we cannot stop labor which we intended on doing but as Nurse Leena stated prior we will be giving you a steroid shot and let labor progress naturally. The longer they are in there the better. Your water hasn't broken yet so there isn't any fear of infection just yet."

I was happy and sad all at the same time, my babies are coming but at what cost, "Dr. Walburn could they die?"

He walked over to the monitor and looked down at the baby's record of their heart beat, "In this day and age Mrs. Collins babies survive at 22 weeks and up and your closer to 31 weeks but with the lack of proper care it's hard to say. One thing for sure their heart beat is strong, these are some fighters."

Dr. Walburn handed nurse Leena the chart, "Give her 12mg of Betamethasone and she shouldn't need a second dose because I don't expect labor lasting over 24hrs."

I looked at both of them confused. That's wasn't a clear answer to me I was still scared. Where is Trey?

 Dr. Walburn walked out the room leaving me in there with Nurse Leena.

She looked over to me, "Honey is there any questions you have for me?

"Yes, what does all this mean?"

"Well for starters Betamethasone is a corticosteroid and it's used for fetal lung development, it increases surfactant which helps the lungs to stay open. For the babies this is good for you just a small side effect of fluid retention and increased blood pressure but less likely to occur at all during such a short period."

"But will they live?"

She looked over her shoulder at the door, "between me and you I think they will be just fine they might have a short stay here but this will surely reduce complications after birth."

Nurse Leena was truly honest and nice and I felt an ounce of relief but just a ounce without Trey being here to hold my hand.

She gave me a reassuring pat on the arm, "I will be back with the shot and do you think you will be in need of any pain medications?"

That was a good question I never even thought about pain medication because deep down I always thought I would have them at the house suffering.

I looked up at her, "I will let you know but Nurse Leena do you know what's going with the Janea the girl in surgery or if anyone else from the house is here."

"I'm not sure the status on anything but I will find out and will let you know when I bring you the shot. Nurse Leena walked out the room. I so bad wanted to get out this bed and find out for myself. I have been waiting on people's answers for almost a year now. Listening and obeying--

Soon a burst of commotion started right outside my door. I could make out Amy and Nurse Leena's voice but it was also another deep male's voice.

I scooted up in the bed moving my head from side to side trying to figure out what was going on through the small glass window then the male voice I now recognized as Detective Louis's voice became clear, "Once he comes to they are both under arrest they were behind this conspiracy too."

I heard Amy's sweet voice become loud, "My husband explained everything. Why are you punishing them?"

Nurse Leena started moving the two of them from in front of the door, "She is in labor take this over there or Detective or not you will be escorted out of my hospital."

What does he mean come to? Who has to come to?

I started yelling at the top of my lungs while pressing the emergency button, "NURSE, NURSE I NEED YOU."

Nurse Leena came running back into the room, "what is it Mrs. Collins?"

"What the hell is going on out there? Have they found my husband? Is he okay?"

"Calm down, you do not need the extra stress."

"I need to know what is going on or I will unhook myself and go find out."

She looked back at the door as though she was silently asking for help and with that look on her face I was freaking out.

She pulled the shot out of her pocket, "I will explain everything but you need this shot so turn to the side.

I did as she said and the shot was inserted right above my buttocks' and a slight pinch and it was over.

Detective Louis finally pushed his way in the room followed by an obviously flustered Amy as Nurse Leena was covering me back up.

"I'm not going to lie to you he said walking closer to the bed. There was a massacre at that house, whoever those people were weren't going down without a fight."

Amy walked over to the chair and sat down her face now clearly with tears. I started hyperventilating. Nurse Leena starting rubbing my shoulder, "breathe Stacy breathe."

"I think this is too much for her please can you wait?" She pleaded with the detective.

I steadied my breathing enough to mumble out a few words, "Where is my husband?"

Before Detective Louis could say another word the door swung open and Detective Karl was standing there with Dr. Walburn.

Detective Karl waved over Detective Louis and they stepped out the room.

I started moving in the bed un-strapping the belts that covered my belly. I wanted to cry out in pain because the contractions were stronger but I fought through the pain because the panic of not knowing what was going on over-ceded those contractions.

Nurse Leena softly pushed me back to the bed, "I know you're worried but you're only going to harm them, take of them and I will take care of you.

I had to admit she was right and she was believable, probably the only person I have believed in years.

I shook my head and she left out the door. I turned in the bed to see Amy's face as white as freshly laid snow.

"Amy what the hell is going on? Where is everyone and what happened to Trey? Please tell me I can't concentrate on them if I don't know what happened to there their dad."

I know I was in a panic and I was throwing out more questions than she could answer but I had to know but Amy just stared out into space.

I put a little more base in my voice and yelled out, "Amy."

She then blinked her eyes and looked over to me.

"He was stabbed by Ma a few times but they say he will make it but he lost a large amount of blood, but that's not the worse part."

Tears started streaming down her face. I kept thinking did something happen to Janea or the other baby.

She set up in the chair because her body was slouched down in the chair with KJ laying flat on her chest sleeping.

"There are a few bodies that need identifying and a few people that are in custody that won't talk."

I gasped, "Bodies."

I knew someone was killed and even though that family had it coming a lot of them were just scared and confused.

I couldn't help though to be relieved that Trey was okay I can't wait to see him and hold him and to tell him I love him even more for what he sacrificed for his children and me.

The door swung open and I nearly pissed my pants being held in cuffs yelling and trying to break free was a bruised and bloody William Barter.

"Get him out of here Detective Louis," Nurse Leena said frantically.

"I need them to identify him he won't talk."

I looked over to Amy and she stood up grasping KJ tight in her arms, she walked slowly over to him and calmly spoke.

"If you truly love her and want to know if she or your babies are okay you will talk."

William stopped moving in Detective Louis grasped and looked clueless to what happened he then spoke, "I am William Barter and could you please tell me what happened to my wife and kids."

Everyone started moving out the room and Amy followed close by.

Nurse Leena walked over to me and looked over at the baby monitor, "they are in distress and if you don't calm down something will happen to them."

She walked over to the door and locked it, "I will tell you everything you want to know then this door will be permanently closed off to everyone, is that understood?"

I looked at the door then at her serious eyes, "Yes."

She walked over to the edge of the bed and sat down, "Here's what I know."

Chapter 27

I'm a mommy now!

The contractions were on top of each other so as Nurse Leena started to talk I was breathing loudly.

"Do you want some pain medication?" she said obviously noticing the pain.

I shook my head no, "Just finish telling me."

She told me there were four male bodies and two women in the morgue and from what Kyle told them two of the children were missing with Ma.

I was crept out by that but she assured me they were keeping an eye out for her besides they don't think she will try anything with the two children she has.

"There is also some wounded women and men in the emergency and we have an officer on each person because we are not sure who are victims and who are perpetrators."

I closed my eyes and let out a hard breathe, "Are any of children hurt?"

She got up from the bed and walked over to the monitor and studied it, "No they have some scrapes and bruises but all of them except the two are accounted for. But I am going to get you some pain medicine you have to sign for it but you obviously need it and I will help with the stress so you can focus on them.

I focused on my breathing and nodded my head. I was determined to do this without the aid of medication but I believe Nurse Leena when she says this will help me.

Nurse Leena walked back to the door first stopping and looking around then she unlocked it, "I will be back in here with Dr. Walburn to check you I have a feeling you have dilated some.

I knew she couldn't lock the door behind her because she wouldn't have looked out to make sure the coast was clear.

I heard the door slowly close behind her so I laid there in the bed doing my breathing techniques and thinking of Trey and how this unfolded wrong. No one was supposed to get hurt or die; they should have been committed in the crazy house. I heard the door open up and instantly knew it was Dr. Walburn I was anxious to see my babies even though this wasn't the life I envisioned.

"Mrs. Collins we will see how far you are before we give you the medication."

I opened my eyes to see Dr. Walburn putting on some gloves. Nurse Leena helped position me in the bed so he could check me. I was so numb to the touch that it was over before I knew it.

Dr. Walburn walked over to the trash and threw his gloves in and gestured his head for Nurse Leena to follow him. She pulled the curtain around the bed and the two of them began to whisper.

I heard the door close and then Nurse Leena walked back around the curtain, "You are dilated to ten which is normal in high levels of stress but only one baby is head down so we will deliver that one first and try to turn the other."

She started pulling things out of drawers and then opened up the ceiling to a mirror and a bright light. The baby incubator that was in the corner of the room she put two little hats in it one pink with yellow stripes and a blue one with white stripes.

Tears started welling up in my eyes I was happy but I didn't want to do this alone I needed Trey. I started to wipe the tears and jumped at the touch of my skin, I forgot the bruise on my face from George Jr. everything started

159

rushing back and I couldn't believe where I was and how I got to this point. I was just a regular high school party girl living it up but I was ahead of my time and that's why I'm here now.

I felt a small pop and then I was peeing on myself.

"Nurse Leena,I think my water broke."

She immediately pulled my gown up, "Yup it's time."

She pressed the call light on the side of my bed, "We need immediate attention in here, baby A is crowning."

Soon after two more nurses came in followed by Dr. Walburn and it appeared to be another doctor, by this time I was breathing erratically.

"Breathe Stacy, breathe." Nurse Leena started chanting.

I heard Dr. Walburn talking to the other doctor while the two other nurses where prepping more equipment.

They pulled out the stirrups and removed the bottom half of the table which made it so I didn't have to slide down, the other nurse lifted the back of my bed while nurse Leena started putting my legs in the stirrups.

I felt like I was in a dream it didn't really seem like in no time I would be holding these little people that I never thought in a million years I would have and even though this wasn't my plan it wasn't their fault and I'm gonna make sure they never feel like they weren't wanted.

I could feel the increase pressure of them right in my vagina since they had me up in the stirrups.

I could hear the door swing open but didn't see anyone because the curtains were drew but I heard a voice, "Stacy, Stacy!"

Amy burst through the curtain with a wave of shock. I could tell she had something to tell me but was caught off guard by the sight of me in the stirrups.

"Oh my God it's time."

I shook my head breathing in and out starting to get aggravated.

"Okay Stacy on the count of three I want you to push as hard as you can," Dr. Walburn looked over at the monitor, "One, two, and three."

I pushed with all my might feeling a slight relief of pressure. Once I pushed out my last breathe I laid back on the bed. The room was silent obviously everyone knew I didn't want to hear anything the loudest thing in the room was the heart monitor for the twins.

Dr. Walburn looked down at my vagina then he pointed to it showing the doctor something.

I let out a hard breathe, "What? What is it?"

Amy put her hands over her mouth and a single tear fell down her cheek, "the head Stacy, the head."

I looked up at the mirror to see a head full of hair coming out my vagina.

"Okay Stacy this little bugger is ready so one more big push on the count of three and Baby A will be in your arms."

Dr. Walburn looked back over at the monitor, "Okay Stacy sit-up because where going to need a big push out of you."

He counted to three and I let out a push so hard that I felt like all my air in my lungs was gone but before I could lay down in defeat the sweet sound of crying flooded the room.

They grabbed some receiving blankets and placed them on my stomach then laid the little one on top of me, my eyes were so watery from crying I could barely see what it was but Amy yelled it out before the doctor had a chance.

"It's a girl."

I can't believe it our baby girl, Trey and mines.

Dr. Walburn placed the scissors in my hand and guided me where to cut her umbilical cord. I gave my baby girl a kiss on the forehead and the nurses took her to be cleaned off and weighed.

"Okay Stacy we have to turn the other one." Dr. Walburn's words echoed in my head.

I braced myself for the pain. I was still having contractions so they waited for one to pass then they did the best they could to turn him.

I whinced out in pain but knew it would be worth it when I saw my baby boy knowing he would look just like Trey.

I wanted to open my eyes but I held them closed so tight that I knew I had water in them because the tears couldn't escape.

I felt someone holding my hand and I knew it was either Amy or Nurse Leena but I didn't care as long as someone was close.

I opened my eyes when I heard the monitor beeping. Everyone including me looked over.

"Oh no baby B heart rate is dropping."

Dr. Walburn ran over to monitor, "We will have to use the forceps or op for a c-section."

I started panicking immediately, "but, but."

I couldn't get out one words the contractions were so hard and I couldn't breathe.

The machine started beeping louder I started breathing louder and louder.

"She is hyperventilating, put her on oxygen now."

Everyone started moving around the room and my head started spinning until I heard Amy's voice in the distance, "Stay with us Stacy, please your baby girl is a healthy 5lbs. 1 oz. Stacy..... Stacy."

Chapter 28

Trey's POV

I stood there holding Ace's hand tight not really wanting to let her go I really wish I didn't do it. I really wish I would have let her go that night but she would be dead right now and probably so would I.

I kept a close eye on Janea, I could already tell she wasn't happy she reminded me of looking at Ace I knew she loved me but it's nothing like having your freedom.

I'm so pissed that they didn't tell me where she was or even how she was doing just forbid us of talking about her and they call us a family no instead they're a psycho unit, well not everyone.

I was hoping the plan would work I hope Pete did what I told him then left because they would torture him to tell who sent him.

The shuffling sound was the only reason I took my eyes of Janea. It was dark but my heart dropped in my chest when I saw him…damn Pete you were suppose to run.

I prayed that he wasn't dead but his body wasn't stiff and I don't think Pa would have brought him over if he was dead.

I stood and watched as he threatened Pete to tell about us but Pete stood his ground and never said a word but I then glanced over to Kyle because even though this wasn't planned this would be the best escape for the girls.

It only pissed Pa off more when Pete told him about his self and how crazy they really were. Once they ran to the back of the house because of the fire I waited patiently for a cue anything. Then the wink, Pete gave it and I knew no one noticed it and then he booked it, he ran so fast I just knew he was going to make it.

I grabbed Janea's hand and unlatched my hand from Ace's then put them together and yelled run from the top of my lungs and they already knew what to do.

Kyle did the same to Amy because of the chaos and now the sirens that were going off I knew they would make it but then BOOM…… "No Pete."

He fell to the ground like a lifeless dummy but I couldn't look but I noticed the girls stopped in their tracks so I yelled for them to run again but that's when I seen the gun straight in my face.

"My own son but you know what I knew it was you."

Pa had me locked in his sights and he would have pulled the trigger if it wasn't for Kyle he jumped Pa and got the gun out his hand, then Pa Barter tried to run up to him Boom the trigger again. The blow back from the gun scared Kyle so he dropped it to the ground but he blew a hole bigger than a pumpkin through him, he was definitely dead. I looked around in the chaos and noticed Harper and Joslynn trying to huddle over the kids by the entrance of the front porch trying their hardest to calm them down. I ran over to my brother who was tussling with Pa and tried to help him. Then I felt it a sharp pain in my side I grabbed it to see blood pouring out and Ma standing behind me, "You ruined everything and to think I gave you the most respect of all my children."

Even though I was bleeding out the words she spoke hit me more. I would have became this if it wasn't for Ace.

I could hear Kyle yelling out my name as my mother stabbed me again and I know she was out her mind but I still managed to get out I love you.

Everything started getting dark but then I seen Kyle tackle Ma down. I knew he didn't want to hurt her but he did get her off of me.

"Freeze or I will shot."

The cavalry finally arrived but was it too late.

I started spitting up blood as my brother lay by my side, "Go make sure our girls made it please forget about me."

He looked down at me and nodded then he bolted out running. I could hear the police yelling at everyone in all directions to freeze but Kyle ran and ran………

I woke up in a cold sweat the sound of machines beeping reminding me where I was as well as what happened. I still lay flat on the bed I could feel the tubes down my throat which made me want to gag. I moved in the bed trying to break free that's when I realized I was cuffed to the bed. The machines started to beep louder and then a nurse rushed in shortly after.

"You're awake, good. If you give me a moment I will get the doctor and we will remove the tubes from you."

She walked out the door but before it could close all the way it swung open nearly hitting the other side of the wall a police officer walked in he was clearly dressed in uniform so there was no mistaking his identity, his face looked so upset that I was scared to be left alone with him. I nearly pissed my pants when he walked closer to me, "Trey Collins we will be talking to you to get the rest of the story when they pull those tubes out."

The rest of the story what happened since I was out? Firstly what day is it and… Ace! Where is Ace?

I would have the answers to my questions shortly because the nurse walked back in the room with an older white man with blue scrubs on that I would assume was the doctor.

"Mr. Collins I'm Dr. Meadows and to take these tubes out I need for you to take a deep breath."

I nodded my head and he put the gloves on and removed the face mask I had on then started gently pulling them out.

Once the tubes were out I instantly without hesitation puked on the side of the bed everyone jumped back besides the nurse, I guess she was used to that kind of thing.

I wiped my mouth with my free hand, "I'm so sorry."

She looked up at me as she was done already cleaning it up, "it's okay son I would have been more surprised if you didn't do it."

The officer was way back in the corner trying to get someone's attention by clearing his throat, "The Detective will want to talk to him now.

Dr. Meadows turned toward the officer, "Could you give us a few we need to make sure our patient is okay before you start bombarding him with questions."

The officer didn't look pleased but he did leave the room.

I didn't give either of them a chance to tell me anything before I blurted it out, "is my wife okay?"

The both exchanged looks as the nurse stood by the sink in the room squeezing out the rag from cleaning up my puke. It only added to the empty pit in my stomach.

She removed her gloves and joined the doctor next to my bed.

"Mr. Collins we won't lie there was indeed a blood bath, we have quite a few bodies in the morgue."

Even though it was terrible news she said it with the sweetest voice.

The doctor walked over to a nearby table and picked up a chart, "We will tell you what we know but first we need to assess your injuries."

I never even thought about myself and what had happened I just needed to know if Ace and our babies were even alive and even thinking about it only brought tears to my eyes.

I reluctantly shook my head.

Dr. Meadows flipped through the pages of the chart, "Your lucky to be alive, we counted about 5 fatal stab wounds most of them hitting a few of your open arteries so who ever stabbed you knew exactly what they were doing. The end result you lost a lot of blood so you will be weak for a while."

I only remember Ma stabbing me twice before I passed out but how did.....

The door busted open again and now there were two gentlemen standing there. The nurse quickly ran to the door, "We are examining our patient you two need to wait out here."

She tried to shuffle them out the room but then the guy with the bald head who was shorter than the other guy spoke, "I'm pretty sure Mr. Collins wants to know how Stacy and his children are doing."

I nearly choked when he said that, "Please! Please! Let them in."

The nurse knew it was too late and they said what I wanted to hear so she stepped away from the door.

Dr. Meadows closed up my chart and walked to the door, "Nurse Susie and I will wait out here push the call button if you require service."

They walked out the door leaving me in the room with the two Detectives.

"Mr. Collins I'm Detective Louis and this is my partner Detective Karl and we have a few questions for you."

"First how is Ace you told me you knew how she was?"

"Your girlfriend is fine last we were in there she was well on her way to deliver those babies."

"Wife, she is my wife!"

Detective Louis walked closer to my bed, "That's what we need to know what made you and your crazy deranged family decide to call these women your wives and keep them locked up?"

I knew he wouldn't understand they just think I'm crazy like them if they only knew it was my life on the line too and Ace would have been dead.

"If I told you, you wouldn't believe me anyways."

Detective Karl walked closer to Detective Louis, "Enlighten us we have heard worse."

I started to explain to them what happened how we got in this heap of a mess they shook their heads while writing down the info but the funny thing is they weren't too surprised.

"I'm kind of getting the feeling you've heard this story before."

Detective Louis put his pad and pen back in his pocket, "Yeah we heard everyone who is coherent version of the story and it seems to match quite a few but a lot of the other ladies wouldn't talk at all."

"Well can you tell me about my wife now?"

Detective Louis looked back at the door, "Just one more question."

I shook my head obviously wanting this to be over.

"Would you know of any whereabouts of your mother she escaped with two of the children we believe from talking to most of the cooperative family members your brother George Jr. and LeAnne Barters children?

I couldn't believe it how did she manage to escape let along take those kids with her.

"I don't know of any safe house all we ever known was our home but wait did you check the Barter's home?"

"Yes we checked every lead we could exhaust that is why there is an officer on every injured family member in the hospital."

I felt bad that I didn't ask about anyone else, I love all my family no matter how crazy but Ace is my heart and without her I couldn't breathe anymore.

I did the best I could to sit up in the bed despite the pain and being handcuffed to the bed.

I lifted my hand, "Are these really necessary?"

Detective Karl walked over to the bed and loosened the cuffs, "Very necessary but now you're comfortable."

"So now you know what's going on can I please get some information?"

Detective Louis took his pad back out his pocket and flipped through the pages, "There are 6 confirmed deaths."

At that moment I didn't want to think about who was dead I knew for sure Pa Barter was dead because Kyle shot him before I even got stabbed by Ma.

Before the Detectives could finish telling me anything else Nurse Susie came back in, "Now I think my patient has had enough questions I really have to check his wounds."

Detective Louis stuffed his pad back in his pocket and the two of them walked out without saying another word.

Once the door closed Nurse Susie walked over to me, "If you stay quiet I will take you to see her because if you love her as much as she loves you there's no way I'm standing in the way of that just call me a romantic."

She headed for the door when I whispered, "But what about----"

I guess she had everything figured out because she turned and put her finger up to her lips.

Even though she had a childlike name Nurse Susie was an older woman with almond color skin and eyes to match her hair was pulled back in a bun and she smiled warmly like a mother should.

She walked out the door but came right back in followed by the officer who stood watch at my door.

"Officer Logan could you possible take these handcuffs off my patient I cannot examine him properly."

The officer looked at me as though he was a little hesitant to do so but he did so anyways.

"I'm not supposed to do this but since you can't go anywhere anyhow, but I'm right outside so no funny business."

Once he was out the room Nurse Susie went in the bathroom and pulled a wheelchair out. I really wonder how she was going to get me out the room with him standing there.

I heard another soft knock on the door and a younger nurse came in the room she had almond color skin with curly brown hair pulled in a pony tail and when she came closer I could see the resembles she had to be related to Nurse Susie because those eyes were a perfect match.

"Okay how are we going to do this?" the younger nurse whispered to Nurse Susie as she helped me off the monitors and out the bed.

I hadn't noticed how she turned the machines off so they wouldn't beep as she unhooked me but she kept me hooked to the IV.

"I'm going to distract him and I want you to take him up there if we get caught I will take the fall."

"But mom,"

"But nothing Leena they shouldn't put these two through this they have been through enough."

She only shook her head and assisted me in the wheel chair.

"When I go outside I will move him closer to the desk and I need for you to stay on me, be watching and here put this on him," she handed her one of those thick hospital sheets.

Nurse Susie walked out the room and Nurse Leena was close on her tail but keeping the distance, she peeped out the door to see how her mom worked her magic then she zoomed me out the door around the corner so fast I thought I would tip out the chair.

Once we made to the elevator she let out her breathe I could tell she had been holding.

"Mother, daughter tag team," I laughed.

She looked over to the elevator panel and pushed number 5, "yeah she can be bossy but sweet and she thinks it was fate that I got Stacy and she got you and I would never argue with that."

It seemed like it took hours for us to go up three floors I love her so much and if she never wants to see me again after this I will be fine I just want to make sure she is okay and so are my babies.

When we reached the floor it was quiet except for a few nurses chatting at the desk then out of nowhere Stacy appears holding KJ she instantly embraces me in a hug, "I'm so happy to see you're okay."

I kissed her on the forehead, "I'm glad you and my nephew are okay, how is Ace?"

She looked up at Nurse Leena and it almost brought tears to my eyes.

She adjusted KJ in her arms and backed back, "I'm going to distract the officer at her door and you guys can go in."

I never noticed how outgoing Amy was I guess surviving what she survived makes someone much more alive.

We stood at the corner until we saw her walk past us Nurse Leena turned me in my chair so I wouldn't be noticed by the officer even though I really didn't think he knew who I was. She wheeled me fast until we reached the door. It seem like it took her forever to open the door she reached over me and twisted the handle and pushed. The curtains were drawn back and the room was quiet except from noise of the machines. I was weak so I couldn't get up to walk over to her so Nurse Leena drew the curtains and my heart stopped she lay there in the bed sleep with an oxygen tubes in her nose and hooked up to every machine the eye could see and right next to her bed an incubator with two small people quietly sleeping next to their mother.

Nurse Leena wheeled me closer to the bed right next to her I pulled my arm up and grabbed her hand rubbing it against my face.

Nurse Leena then walked over to the other side of the bed where the twins were, "she is in a coma, we did everything we could but baby B was breeched and because she was under so much strain so was he his heart dropped and so did hers then she started hemorrhaging so we rushed her to the OR where we delivered him cesarean and delivered the placenta that was the problem but because not enough oxygen was going to her brain she slipped in a coma. The doctors aren't sure if it's permanent or not.

I lay my head next to her head on the bed. I did this to her and will we ever be a family? Will she be able to hold these little people she fought so hard for?

One of the babies started to cry it was soft and low not loud how I would imagine so Nurse Leena picked her up she was wrapped tight in the blanket but she had on a pink and yellow striped hat on. She walked her over to me and I couldn't help but to be nervous, I mean I've held babies I have a load of nieces and nephews but to hold your own well I will see.

She gently placed her in my arms and right at that moment my heart melted just peering in those light hazel eyes I knew she was daddy's little girl.

I only got a moment with my little girl when the door swung open, "How dare you, you psycho touch my granddaughter or her babies."

Mrs. Bellows grabbed my little girl out my arms and soon after Detective Louis and Detective Karl came rushing in the room as they were pushing me out Ace's heart monitor started beeping.

Nurse Leena called a code red and the room was filled in seconds with staff one who started pushing us out the room but not before the doctor yelled out she's flat lining. I grabbed my chest at that moment I felt someone ripping my heart out nothing could stop me from running over to her bed.

"Ace please don't leave us I promise you will never again fear for your life, you will always be loved and took care of just please don't ---

I was pulled off of her by the Detectives while her grandmother yelled to me it's your doing if she dies.

Dies? If she dies so will I. I won't live without her.....

Chapter 29

Stacy/Ace/ Is it finally over?

I opened my eyes slightly they were so heavy I couldn't completely open them so I scanned the room and nothing about this room seemed familiar although my eyes weren't all the way open. Everything was blurry like I was walking through a fog I really couldn't make out anything but I did hear a beeping sound over, and over, and over again it was starting to get annoying. I tried to talk but no words came out my mouth, it was dry as cotton so I moved my hand to get any kind of sense of what was going on. I felt a hand I turned my head slightly in the direction of the hand and it was grandma sleeping .Then like a flash of lightning it all came crashing back in my head and that's when I flew up, "Trey!"

Grandma jumped out her sleep, "Oh child you startled me. It's okay no one can hurt you now."

I swung my legs over the side of the bed and winced in pain I felt on my belly suddenly realizing it was a small scar with stitches, "My babies, Grandma are my baby's okay?"

Grandma walked over to the side of the bed my legs were dangling and lifted me back in, "Stacy I'm going to need you to stay put before you bust a stitch."

"I really don't care," Still continuing to get out the bed. "I need to see my babies."

She looked at me like she was puzzled, "Why would you want the rapist babies?"

I nearly slapped her but I held my composure.

"Grandma what on earth would possess you to think Trey was a rapist."

She started rubbing my leg like she did when she had to break some bad news to me as a child.

"Didn't he kidnapped you and force himself on you?"

"No Grandma he saved me if it wasn't for him, Pa…I mean George Collins Sr. would have killed me. I was going down a terrible path as you know blaming everyone for my problems and shielding the ones who loved me from helping me if he didn't pick me as his mate I would be as sure as dead right now, you see Pa might have been a lunatic but I learned that we have choices in life and it's all up to us as to how we use them."

I was out of breath from saying it so fast hoping she would just let me go.

Grandma put her hand over her mouth like you do when you're in shock then I saw her eyes get watery. I wasn't quite sure why she was tearing up but I knew it was a good things.

"I'm sorry baby, after your momma died I tried my best to heal you but the pain ran too deep but right now, here on this day your heart is healed. I've never heard you speak in this way."

I grabbed grandma's hand, "granny you did your absolute best and I sure don't blame you, it was something within me and it was something forced out of me too, I now see I took your love and everyone else's for granted I was so damaged that I couldn't see that love was right in front of me all that time. I still maintain I was ahead of my time. I promise you one thing grandma I will protect and love the twin's right and I know Trey will be a good father."

Grandma's eyes shifted a little then she gently slid her hand out of mine.

"I'm going to call your friend Amy in here while I give the Detectives a call."

"Grandma where's Trey and my babies?"

She slowly made her way to the door, "The babies are fine but…I will be right back."

She was out the door before I could call her any further so I reached around the bed again and found the call light hanging over the side of the railing.

"I need a nurse in here now please."

Not more than a minute passed before three familiar faces were coming through the door, nurse Leena and Amy holding a smiling KJ.

Amy came and plopped on the bed while nurse Leena started checking my vitals.

"You just don't know how worried we were, you were out cold," Amy said leaning in to hug me.

"How long was I out? What happened to everyone? Where is Trey?"

"Whoa slow it down," Nurse Leena said while trying to suppress her laughter.

We both looked back at her while she was grabbing the blood pressure cuff thinking nothing was funny about the situation.

She looked up at us, "I'm not trying to be disrespectful but you didn't give the girl a chance to answer one question."

She was right I just need to know what's going on. I'm still in shock that this even happened.

Amy rolled her eyes then jumped off the bed while KJ stayed content and quiet he is definitely a good baby.

"First off everyone is in jail, protective custody whatever you would call it because upon investigation they found over a 100 bodies on that land but the freaky thing is some were decades old."

Amy walked over to the chair to take a seat, her face now an obvious frown.

"The good news is Janea is ok although she is in a coma as you were and her twins are just fine but the doctors said she will not be able to have any more children if she even wakes up."

"Well Excuse me," Nurse Leena smiled politely, "Are you ready to see your new edition on that note?

What did she think of course I wanted to see my baby's?

 "Yes bring them in," I said anxiously.

Nurse Leena walked out the room, only to walk right back in with a wheelchair.

"Hun, they are in Neonatal, although their weights were okay for the delivery date, baby A couldn't keep her temperature up, and baby B the one we had to deliver by emergency c-section could not breathe on his own. They were fine for a few hours but couldn't sustain alone, so we moved them."

I lost my breath. I knew everything couldn't be perfect but the important thing is they're alive.

Amy got out of the chair and walked toward the door while Nurse Leena helped me out the bed. Once I was situated in the wheelchair we walked silently down a few halls then on the elevator down two floors from where my room was. Nurse Leena swiped her ID badge when we reached two double doors to get access through them. After going down the longest hallway ever she swiped her badge one more time, then the doors opened to a floor similar to the one I was on but the difference was most of the rooms had cribs instead of beds.

"This is Stacy Collins to see her twins."

The older looking nurse with a not so nice look on her face picked my arm up and scanned my wrist bands. I hadn't even noticed the three bands that were on my wrist, one said my name on it with my birthday and sex, and the other one had baby boy Collins with the sex and birthday and same for the other one it just said baby girl Collins.

We quietly walked down a hall not too far from the nursing desk; the nurse looked back down at my wrist band then walked in a room we stopped in front of.

There were butterflies forming in my stomach I was excited but I couldn't help feel this wasn't right Trey should be here holding my hand instead of Amy although I am grateful she is here.

The frumpy looking nurse waved us in the room; I instantly noticed which baby was which my son was in an open incubator with tubes around his nose and another one down his throat and my daughter's incubator was a little different it looked like she was in a small oven. Once we were all in the room the older nurse opened up my daughter's incubator she grabbed some blankets from under the table then she gentle picked her up one handed and wrapped her tight in the blankets and gently placed her in my arms. I could feel my body warm up or was it my heart melting.

"She is so beautiful Stacy she looks like a little you." Amy gushed.

Even though she was little you could see those features coming through and she would definitely be a looker just like her mommy.

"Trea'sa Janelle Collins, that's her name."

Amy bent down to get a closer look at her, "When did you come up with that."

I glided my hand across he smooth face, "In a dream. Trey and I didn't have time to come up with any names but this name is just right and a perfect fit for her because it means strong."

"Well I guess that was 2 weeks well spent coming up with a name."

I looked back up at Amy realizing she meant I was in a coma for two weeks.

I spent a few hours down in the nursery with Trey Jr. and Trea'sa I didn't want to leave but Nurse Leena insisted on me eating and Amy never left my side except to tend to KJ.

I was alone in my room for the first time today and I sat at the edge of the bed glaring out the window at the dark blue sky with the moon shining brighter than I ever seen. I was at ease for that moment even with all the chaos going on in my life I just knew everything was going to be alright.

The door slide open and I knew it could only be 1 of 3 people who have been in and out my room all day. I turned in the direction of the door and my heart nearly dropped, standing in the doorway wasn't Nurse Leena, grandma, or even Amy but the love of my life. I jumped off the bed knowing full well I would pay for it later and ran to Trey faster than the wind could take me. I leapt in his arms and he squeezed me so tight for just that moment I forgot how we got here, the murders, the kidnapping everything was perfect and then our silent embrace was ruined.

My face was ducked off in Trey's chest but I could hear the bad imitation of someone trying to clear there throat.

"Mrs. Collins I'm so happy to see you're okay."

I couldn't move out the warmth of Trey's chest nor did I want to and even though he hasn't been at the coffee house for a while I can smell ground coffee beans on him and it assures me things are going to be just fine.

I lifted my head up just slightly to see Detective Karl and Detective Louis standing behind Trey.

Trey gently lifted me up in his arms cradling me like a baby, "Ace you just delivered twins, and I will feel much better if you were lying down."

"I had 2 weeks to heal I just want to be close to you."

Trey could never tell me no so he carried me to the bed and laid down with me both of us didn't even pay attention to the Detectives walking closer to the bed.

It was late so it made me wonder why they were even here, "So what's going on? Did you clear everything up?"

Detective Karl gazed out at the night sky, "Three things cannot be long hidden: the sun, the moon, and the truth. Buddha."

There really was no explanation for it he said it with that quote, everything was over and Trey was cleared and it took two weeks to do it.

Trey kissed me on the forehead and stroked my check, "Everything is over Ace now we can take our twins home and be safe, happy and free!

I had so many unanswered questions but at this moment when Trey said free I trusted him and knew everything was over.

Hopefully.

Chapter 30

2 months later/ A Brighter Future

I woke up to brightest sun in the sky. I laid flat for a moment taking in the silence then I quickly got wondering why it was so quiet, the twins should have been up by now. I moved my hand around in the bed and realized why, Trey must have got them. I stretched a bit and walked over to the bathroom it felt good to look like myself with just puffy eyes from being sleep deprived but it was worth it. I made my way to the nursery which was only right next to our room it wasn't no way I was being inches away from them let along down the hallway. I walked in the beautifully decorated nursery, Trey really out did himself the top half of the wall was painted a teddy bear brown while the bottom half had pink, blue, and brown stars all around, both cribs were up against the wall with a huge letter of the first initial hung over the wall, the bedding was brown with pink boarders around them for Trea'sa, and blue for TJ. I truly loved the room and he did it quickly because we only been in this house for two weeks. The whole process with the funeral and money being tied up took 6 weeks because technically the heir to the money was still alive which was Ma aka Cecilia Collins it took a long process for the children to inherit there huge family dynasty which I couldn't believe they were sitting on, actually Trey and Kyle couldn't believe it themselves their families combined net worth was in the hundred millions.

Trey was in the middle of the room rocking Trea'sa the diva in the rocking chair, even at two months old she knows she's daddy's little girl. The twins were released the day after we moved in that's why Trey did their room so quickly their hospital stay seemed like forever I was up there all day every day for those six weeks crying most times when I had to leave them. The hospital kept extra staff on them because of Ma being on the loose and her extent knowledge on a lot of things so they didn't want her to get away with either set of twins although the police were sure she was going to lay low for months until things blew over but Trey, Kyle, Amy, Janea, William and I knew way better than that. Trey and Kyle hired extra help and security guards but I assisted on taking care of my kids myself so they mainly just cook and clean. I know it seems weird but we decided to stay together because we had been each other's crutch as well as Trey wanted to be close to his sister because of her being gone for 3 years and keeping an eye on William Barter which I understood because I didn't fully trust him myself.

"I see the lil Diva has you wrapped around her little finger this morning."

Trey looked up from gazing at her and smiled at me. I slowly walked over to TJ's crib and he was peacefully sleeping away.

"I already fed him and put him back to sleep so if you want to lie back down."

I walked over and kissed Trey on his forehead, "I will make you some breakfast you're far too good to me."

I proceeded down the stairs of the 3 story house, the house was just as big as Ma and Pa's house but it was closer in town I think the guys knew we would be scared living away from people since we had been secluded for so long.

I could smell the aroma of breakfast already being prepared and knew it was no other than Amy.

"Good morning Amy." She looked up from the stove as she was flipping pancakes."

"Did you sleep well," She said smiling at me."

"I slept like a baby considering Trey got the twins when they woke up."

I walked over to the stove and gave her a hug, "Where's Janea?"

"I haven't seen her or William this morning."

Janea had been a little depressed when she came home because of the hysterectomy they had to give her; she had been distant from the twins which had caused for everyone else to pick up the slack. Trey and Kyle spoke to William about getting her some help like we did for the trauma and the seclusion. Although I don't know how much help they could have been since our therapist diagnosed Amy and I with Stockholm syndrome and assisted we leave them.

We have been getting a lot of negative feedback from the press our families and a shit load of people about staying with the guys but no one would never know what we endured in my year and Amy's two years. They shouldn't really judge.

I looked out the window to see if William's truck was in the driveway and didn't see it so it got me worried.

I heard footsteps coming down the stairs and it was Kyle and Trey Kyle was holding KJ. Once they got to the bottom of the stairs Kyle let KJ free, he has been crawling everywhere they had to baby proof the house as soon as we moved in.

We all sat at the table to have breakfast , everyone was eerily quite I think the guys thought the same thing Amy and I had been thinking about William, although William was a Barter he was cool but a bit distant.

We all stared at each other for the longest exchanging looks for one person to the next until the door opening broke the staring contest and eerie silence. All attention went to the door as William stood in the doorway with some grocery bags. Instantly Kyle and Trey got up to help him.

"Thanks guys," he smiled warmly at them.

Both me and Amy exchanged looks, it wasn't that he was rude it just seemed as though he was truly sincere.

I got up from the table, "So what goodies are in there?" I said waving my head side to side to look in the bags.

The guys made their way to the dinette table while William started removing things from the bag.

"Just some of Janea's favorite foods and things, I'm trying to get her out of her mood."

"Great idea," Both Kyle and Trey said at the same time.

The two of them had a smile from ear to ear and I got it they loved their sister and if he was trying to make her happy he was alright in their book.

Amy and I cleared the table smiling, and I feeling like everything was going to be okay.

The day turned into night before we knew it, the four of us were playing with the kids and just enjoying life, we hadn't heard from William or Janea all day but we just needed to give them some time to their selves. Janea had to adapt just like we do to freedom.

KJ started getting fussy so Amy and Kyle excused themselves for bed time leaving Trey, I and the twins in the den watching T.V until the T.V. started watching us.

I instantly jumped up when I heard a crashing sound. I looked around the room and Trey was laid out on the floor next to Trea'sa bouncer and TJ was fast asleep in the swing. I thought to myself I must have been dreaming but then I heard it boom, boom. After that there was no need to wake Trey he jumped up.

"What the hell was that?"

I looked at him shrugging my shoulders. We were to the far left of the house the den was secluded so you would have to walk through the foyer, the library and the sitting room to get there so the sound was muffled.

"I'm going to see what it is Trey whispered."

"No babe you stay with the kids it's probably nothing."

"Are you crazy Ace I'm not going to let you off by yourself," he said lifting his self off the floor.

"Trey please don't make me argue with you, first of all we have security surrounding this place it can't be anything serious."

Trey scratched his head and me knowing full well what it meant he was never able to tell me no unless my life was in danger but it didn't sound like much danger with the constant security surrounding us.

"I'm only feet away holler if it's anything funny."

I nodded my head and slowly walked to the door I turned around again and looked Trey in his eyes.

"If you do hear anything the kids are your number one priority."

Trey listened to me to a certain point but he knew I was right at the end of the day it was me or them and I would lay my life down for them.

I tiptoed through all the rooms not hearing a word but once I got to the sitting room that no one really sits in I seen a shadow standing by the stairs, now that was creeping just when I was about to tiptoe back to Trey I heard a familiar voice.

"Your tyranny is over and you no longer run our lives."

I ran into the foyer to see one body close to the door and Janea standing over a lady holding her hands in defense while Janea pointing an already smoking gun at her.

I screamed at the top of my lungs because I knew that would be the only way everyone would come running. I was glued in my tracks.

It seemed like hours passed but in mere seconds Trey was next to me with two hollering babies one in each arm it was like he just snatched them up and ran as fast as the wind could take him.

186

What's going on he said bending over trying to catch his breath. I slowly lifted my arm up and pointed to Janea. Then out of the blue William tackled Janea to the ground the gun flipped out her hand and slide right in front of me. Amy and Kyle came running down the stairs. Amy switched on the light right at the bottom of the stair case. Our eyes grew wide when we saw the horror, it wasn't just any person it was Ma in the flesh and by the look of her, Janea already wounded her but by the door was one of the guards the guys hired.

"Shoot her Stacy; Shoot her all the shit we have been through we will finally be free SHOOT HER." Janea yelled from up under William.

I slowly picked the 9mm up grasping it and remembering going to the shooting range almost every day the twins were in the hospital then everything started rushing through my head all at once being kidnapped, Pa beating me, constantly being scared. Then time seemed to slow and looking at her as she lifted from the ground holding her wounded side smiling like Pa would, then I turned slowly looking at my babies and then Trey but in a matter of seconds she rushed me and BOOM!

I dropped the gun to the ground as Ma fell to her knees clinching her chest or rather her heart. I always wondered if she knew she was shot there or was it the fact that her heart was truly broken. I saw the key that dangled around her neck and bent down, "Here's our key to freedom." then snatched it from her neck.

In all the time we thought it was William Barter keeping in touch with Ma it was Janea. Everything she went through she knew it was Ma and not Pa so the depression was from knowing she was still alive so she hired one of her henchman or brainwashed men or whatever you would call them as our guards to reel her in but after everything was said and done only the 6 of us ever knew the truth of how she set Ma up and we kept it that way. As for the rest of the surviving family members we only ever see Joslynn. Trey says he doesn't know if it's that they don't forgive us or they just don't know how to live anymore.

I'm an inspiring writer from Grand Rapids, Michigan. I've been writing since 14 but really got serious about my writing 3 years ago and have been determined ever since. I'm a busy mother of 7 beautiful girls and have been residing in Michigan all my life. I plan on working on more wonderful stories in the near future.

Kendra Armstrong
AHEAD OF MY TIME